Vera's Still Point

RUTH PERKINSON

Spinsters Ink
2006

Spinsters Ink, Inc.
P.O. Box 242
Midway, FL 32343

Printed in the United States of America on acid-free paper
First Edition

Editor: Anna Chinappi
Cover designer: LA Callaghan

ISBN 1-883523-73-7

For my sister and best friend, Mary Kathryn Perkinson, and my mother, Sue Perkinson—both angels of light in my hours of greatest darkness.

Acknowledgments

Many gracious thanks go to Leila Christenbury, Professor of English at Virginia Commonwealth University, who read aloud a story about my father one day in class many years ago. I became a teacher because of you.

My apologies for the nearly one thousand students I taught in Henrico County Schools for almost ten years. I never mentioned the word homosexuality, ever. This book is for the ones I could have helped more but was paralyzed into staying silent by my own fear and shame.

Thanks to the faculty of both schools where I taught—especially Mary Jane Huffman, Vicki Ragland, Hilary Raymond and Anne Poates: steadfast pillars of support.

My family—my mother and father, sister and brother (and his family) for all their love. My uncle Ron who made me believe in God again. My friends—Leigh Ann, Kim, Mandy, Amy, Erin, Patrice, Krista, Rebecca, Art, and especially, Julie.

Warm regards to Linda Hill and my editor, Anna Chinappi.

A very special acknowledgement goes to Susan Gencarelli who at nineteen died in a car crash when I was only twelve years old. She brought me to this.

About the Author

Ruth Perkinson lives in Richmond, Virginia, with her two dogs, Scout and River.

Chapter 1

I was stronger than I thought.

When I was nearly forty years old, I got into the second fistfight of my life, my second bloody nose. The first one happened in third grade when Pete Van Hedron and his gang had put fists full of black spiders down the back of my shirt as a rite of passage. Their theory was to scare the hell out of me, and then I was either in or out of their club, depending. Frenetic and frazzled, it took me two hours to calm down after flailing my arms and hands wildly at their faces, missing them because I was blind from tears that ran in spurts down my chubby face. One punch from Peter had landed on my nose, and the blood, sweat and tears had fogged the lenses of my glasses.

Later that night, I felt a spider crawling on my face as I lay asleep, and I jumped into my sister's bed and didn't stop sleeping with her for nearly two years. She didn't mind as long as I slept only on the six inches closest to the wall and didn't touch her. No problem. Later, in therapy, I discovered a theme coloring my life as panic and anxiety conjoined with the spider metaphor: Always they lay in my vision, always the dreams were jungles full of them—darting, crawling, jumping at my feet, legs, hands, arms and head. Sometimes they were slow, sometimes fast, but always hairy and black as pitch. They morphed their faces into evil people with tarantula-red eyes and stilted legs and bulbous bodies as big as Brazil. They chased me my whole life.

Rites of passage can be costly.

The first bloody nose came at the price of my fragile mind. The second one came at a much higher price—the right to watch my girlfriend die. Her name was Frankie Bourdon. Frankie Bourdon was dying, and I hadn't had a girlfriend in over ten years and not ever one the likes of her. School teaching and my own self-conscious sterility had been the bane of my existence. It all happened that day, that year, because in the Commonwealth of Virginia, House Resolution Bill 751 had been born again. A bill created to impose a law that restricted people like me—homos—from doing things like marrying, drawing wills and visiting one's lover in the hospital, God forbid. We homos were abhorrent—by nature, by God, but especially by the laws of Virginia. I agreed. Eleven hundred laws against homosexuals in the great Commonwealth, and I agreed with them all.

Except for Easter in the year 2000.

The day was a canvas of faded watercolors, the way the sky lit itself in its own iridescent pall of pink and purple. The illumination had cast a shadow over the Catholic edifice of St. Mary's hospital in Richmond, Virginia. On that day I held the theater of my own court at the entranceway to the hospital. There was me, Vera Curran, dressed in manly drag. I looked like Captain Kirk in the bay of his Starship Enterprise with my black Reeboks and gold shirt and painted black sideburns. I was "married" to Brock Goldberg at the time. Brock was a great fag dressed in drag who also happened to be my girlfriend's best friend. He donned his favorite drag recipe—Barbra Streisand. I should have been James Brolin, a better fit perhaps, but Captain Kirk it was, and Captain Kirk I did.

Then there were Lucy McGillicutty and Alma Lourdes, my best friends, watching my back like they had always done. Two gems in the roughest part of my life. And, like a fickle spider, there she was, Eileen Bourdon, Frankie's mother. There as she had been from the inception of the deception. There to watch her daughter die. My dark-haired Frankie Bourdon with her thin statuesque body who lay in Room 514 dying of the cancer in her lungs and bones. But the cancer was much deeper than that.

Eileen Bourdon, whose own jaw was clenched while the muscles at the intersection of her lower mandible and lower ear lobe bulged from nights of clenching, nights of thinking, arrived at the scene with her partner in Christian crime, Paul Winterfield. They both met me at the front of the entranceway to the hospital. I had eyed her from the moment she emerged from her powdery white Suburban. Her gait took on long strides, and her feet sported black semi-stiletto pumps sharp like her nose, and her fire-red hair stood straight up on end and lay all around her like a burnt-out halo. A blue suit from Nordstrom's outlined her bulbous belly and her sagging sixty-year-old breasts. Tired out from her tirades, I stood there. She walked up to me, and put her hands on her hips. I tugged at my shirt then did the same in my mocking way.

Her own life as a lady of Three Chopt Avenue had been marred by a cheating husband and raising two children.

Frankie, the youngest, turned out to be homosexual in the middle of Eileen's born-again crisis. Eileen was halfway into the laws of Leviticus when Frankie came home from a beer party at eighteen, threw up and proceeded to say, "What would Jesus say if I told you I was gay?" It took Eileen only a nanosecond before she smacked her across the face with the very Bible she was holding and spanked her all the way up the stairs yelling, "Jesus would want you to get to your room and not come out till you redeemed yourself." Eileen apologized twelve years later by giving Frankie an orchid to put by her bed in the hospital. It was the one act that gave Frankie faith that Jesus might just be a little pissed instead. But, Frankie did not know much about Jesus, just that he and the Bible and her mother had mixed up hell and heaven and havoc to the point where it was suffused into her skin like cement.

"Well," she said. I looked at Brock who stood five feet behind me. He wiped lipstick from his lips, which smeared across his cheek. Lucy and Alma were coming out of the doors to greet us when I said the words that made Eileen slap me across the face.

"Hey, Eileen. Got Jesus yet or just a dying dyke?"

When we headlocked, we became an intertwined yin and yang. She tore out some of the wisps of my thin black hair, half-bald as I was, and with my pudgy fingers I tore out red tufts from her head to litter the sidewalk. I would have evidence for my friends that I still had some fight in me, even though I had been an outsider for the whole homo movement, especially the movement Frankie had been behind—the right to teach about homosexuality in schools. The cause. Yuk. Give me a good night with Shakespeare and *Richard the Third* and, well, there's a goddamned cause.

Eileen and I pulled and pulled like two high school girls fighting over a boyfriend. I flailed like an asthmatic banshee and whirled her like a dervish till she may have made it in the paper for the next best ride at King's Dominion. A commercial headliner for sure—*Baldheaded Bitch of a Ride*. That's what I would have called it. The scuffle lasted only thirty seconds but seemed suspended in time. Lucy and Alma and Brock yelled at us to stop. I responded between grunts and pulls by telling them to break into song like from *West Side Story*. Eileen had the best of me in her headlock till I managed to put the death grip on her right nipple. It wouldn't have been so bad if I had used my hand, but with the way she had me pinned, the only way out was to bite. And bite hard I did. She screamed that I was a freak with my freak-show entourage and ran back to her car with one pump on.

"Just pretend you're an Amazon, Eileeeen!" I yelled after her. "They didn't need their right tits anyway. Next time, just shoot me with a goddamned bow and arrow." I spat out my disgust for her on the ground. We all lingered while Alma tended to my nose. Just as I was getting into Brock Goldberg's car, the police arrived and placed me under arrest. I kept pointing to my nose, (I later found out her nipple had gotten the worst of it) but I knew then that I had screwed up my last chance to ever see her daughter again. Frankie Bourdon—my gravest mistake. It was Frankie who got me in the whole damn predicament in the first place.

If you ask me, I really don't know the truth about how it had come to this. The millennium had had an impact on everyone, me included. Computers and terror threats and duct tape had all commingled into one gigantic American panic attack. The description of it all half-eluded me as I thought this out.

The air was thick then like it was the morning I began to tell my 21-year-old nephew Kyle the story. A haughty Virginia mist crept over the dark shallows of the farming valley where

I lived. Just forty minutes west of Richmond, Louisa was a small conservative county that prided itself on the good ol' boy network. Hell, most of the state prided itself on it.

From Highway 250, one could jet west to find the rural tract by following the James River and the cadence of the country road, which itself runs parallel to the train tracks all the way from the Norfolk shipyard to Kalamazoo, Michigan. I had driven the road a million times, back and forth between the City of the Monuments to my simple country home. Always the same road, always the same way. The county roads slide like a linear carousel with slow rises and slow dips where dairy farms and horse farms make up the lining and framework. And between all of that, one can see Civil War markers reminding everyone that Dixie was the place to be even if we did lose the goddamned war. Rebel flags and bumper stickers that said, "The South's Gonna do it Again" still remained signs that ignorance and bigotry were alive and well. I should know having taught half the county eleventh-grade English before I made the transition to become a librarian to set myself free from the fetters of the redneck classroom where crew cuts and big hair and blue eye shadow and soiled boots and moonshine forebears sat rowed up in front of me like an Illinois cornfield for over fifteen years.

The transition from teacher to librarian came for me at Louisa High School in the fall of 1998. It was the same year Frankie Bourdon came to our faculty as the newest physical education teacher and basketball coach. The incumbent PE teacher, Elsie Moses, had left in late August over stolen money and sex. Apparently, it finally came out that Elsie had been pilfering money through bogus fund raisers and was caught passing love notes to some girl on her basketball team just the season before—a senior on her way to play at UVA. I had felt sorry for Elsie. Like me, she was in what I call the flannel dyke category—short haircut just above the ears, white golf shirts, khaki pants and black Reeboks. She was heavy and puffy like me and smoked and drank ice cold beer every night with a TV dinner, so naturally I had an affinity for her. She was the best defensive back for the BackStreet Girls flag football team. Each year in Key West she would win some kind of outstanding award for either Beers the Most Drunk or Drunk with the Most Beers. When she asked me once if I wanted to play, I told her that I wasn't much good at blocking and knocking around and such. She slapped me on the back and said, "I'll teach you, Curran." Truth was, I didn't much want to hang around a bunch of flannel dykes. The other category was much more appealing to me—lipstick lesbians or just "lipsticks." Elsie said that it was the nineties and that the lipsticks came out to play, too. I said sorry. Anyway, old Elsie hung up her gym shoes and began writing the history of lesbian flag football while bartending at my favorite pub. Three months after her dismissal, I'd never seen her happier.

Frankie in, Elsie out. That was when the trouble began.

Six months after the scene of the crime in front of the hospital, I recapped my diatribe with Kyle. He was mine for the weekend and needed help in Psychology 201. He thought that some of my psycho-diabolical tale would help him get an A on a paper about homosexuality—seemed to be a hot topic, and he needed his aunt to testify about how she used to hate the subject and now how it wasn't so bad after all. He also liked to visit when he and his father weren't getting along. Laundry was part of the deal, too. Aunt Vera—always good for beer, talk and plenty of Tide. The assignment was an excuse to get away.

He flew into my driveway I'm certain as fast as he drove the highway with the smoke and dirt rising like a parachute. It followed him all the way till he stopped. When he emerged from the car, I couldn't believe how he had morphed from baby fat to young man in the last few years. The dirty blond hair is muffed up all over his head and his button-fly jeans half way down to his knees. He took a long stretch, then came slowly up my brick walk, taking easy steps.

Even though he was my brother's son, I do not look like I am related to him. The Curran house had shut its good-looking door on me and hit me with the ugly stick. I do not care so much about that anymore, but for a long while, I found that it affected me greatly. My mud brown eyes were too close together, and the right one sagged a little when comparing and contrasting in the mirror—something I've done with my buddy Lucy. My head sat atop my frame as if I were an upside-down exclamation point with my body screaming to get off of me. My neck was long and crepey, and my cheeks were drawn in and scarred from teenage acne. I had even but gapped teeth and my dark mouse-brown hair was bowl cut number nine on the Tupperware line—straight, thin, flat and short, a Davy Jones imitation from 1965. Depending on the time of the month and the number of beers drunk, my weight ranged between 165 and 172. I was five-foot-four and slew-footed. I was the epitome of black and white flannel dyke. Color-blind, I could not have matched an outfit even if Lucy McGillicutty had the Garanimal tags laid out side by side before me.

My small brick home was not far from Richmond, right off Highway 250, almost equidistant from it and Louisa High School. Nestled on a small ridge, the front yard was sparsely wooded in the front, maples mostly, but the sixty-year-old pines leaned precariously over the edges of slate roof in the back. The front porch had a bowl for Grace (one in the back, too) appropriately named "dog." And, of course, there was my American flag waving in the ripples of an almost always-incandescent Virginia sky. It stayed out year round, a never-ending theme on letting freedom ring, Fourth of July style—a tribute to Frankie Bourdon's favorite holiday, a tribute to my Republican days of yore.

But, it was September in Louisa, Virginia. It was cool outside, and Frankie had been dead since Easter. Jobless for the first time in over twenty years, I welcomed my nephew with his laundry and his questions and maybe his moments of suspended disbelief.

"Aunt Vera! How are you?" He stepped in a hole where Gracie-Mac had dug and tripped halfway up the walk.

I laughed. "Are you okay? Why are you yelling?" I hammered back.

"What?" he said.

"Why are you yelling!"

Gracie-Mac, my yellow lab adorned with rainbow collar, ran to greet him. Her tail half hit her head each time she did the skippity-skip body wag for him. Had an affinity for the boy, I reckoned.

"You've lost weight, Kyle. Here, hand me your bag."

"What did you say?" he asked, handing me the bag. "Did you say I was losing weight?" He snuffled his dusty nose and patted ol' Grace. The body wag continued, the tail lethal on his legs. "Here, give me a hug. It's good to see you."

"No, I said you look like Tom Cruise. Now stop squeezing me so hard, you'll bust a rib." I broke away from him and looked at his hair. Jesus. Then to his ears. "What's that hanging off your ears?"

He pulled at them. "They're my new hoops. Like 'em?"

I patted Gracie. "Well, I guess so. Does your dad like them?" I asked, then scratched my side and tugged at my white T-shirt.

"He doesn't know I have them pierced. I take them off when he's around. Do you have anything to drink." He migrated into my kitchen. The refrigerator was opened, and he rifled through my stash of food and drink.

I plopped down on the sofa. "Don't touch the beer. If you want to write this paper, I don't want you getting anything screwed up. Your professor will think you're not my nephew if you get the syntax and semantics all in a dilly over being drunk."

No peep from the kitchen. I heard him pop a top. Then into my living room, "Now, Aunt Vera. Where should we begin?" He had a beer and plopped beside me on my leather couch. All plops completed.

"Have the piercings screwed up your hearing?"

"No, why?"

"Just checking. Do you need some paper or something? Laptop? I'd offer mine up except it's at the store getting some new hardwire or whatever it needs. I can't remember."

Kyle took a long, slow drink of beer then shook his head and said he'd just use a voice recorder and amend the rest on his own laptop. He looked at me. He really did look a bit like a movie star, I thought. A twenty-year-old ladies man, I was sure. His olive skin was like his mother's and blue eyes and sandy hair like his dad's. Strong arms and skinny legs and silver rings and black bracelets hung on him in an attempt at ornamentation.

"Does Jack know you're drinking beer and hanging out with his lesbo-a-go-go sister for the next few days?" I said, and leaned back to rest my head. I took his beer, sipped it, then gave it back.

Kyle winked at me. "Dad knows I'm out of town, but I left

it at that." He took out his recorder and placed it on the coffee table. I stared at it and paused. This was hard—sitting in my living room and trying to remember all that had gotten me here. There was a pause as I looked through my bay window to remember, remember the desolation of how people get caught up in ideas and power and religion.

Our eyes are like cameras, Frankie had once said to me. I smiled at her image in my head.

"Come on, Aunt Vera! Let's get started. I'll keep my whereabouts a secret. Anyway, what the old pecker doesn't know isn't going to hurt him." I told Kyle that I wasn't sure where the beginning laid itself out, how it truly all got started.

"I don't care," he said. "Just start from the beginning."

"Okay, turn it on."

For nearly twenty years, I managed to stay a good ol' girl. I had my two best friends, Alma Lourdes and Lucy McGillicutty. Alma was a former buddy from my college years and an art teacher at Freeburg High School in Richmond. Tall and lanky, Alma wore thick reading glasses that were eternally slipping down her nose. She pushed them up about every fifteen seconds with her middle finger which always made me think she was telling the world to screw off in a subliminal way. She was too shy and reserved to know that this was the case. Even though she was forty-three years old, the acne still covered her face. Her school-marmish clothes hung on her frame, and she was about as coordinated as a one-armed midget stacking cans of corn on the top shelf. Ol' Alma always trying to be the comic in the group, but it was Luce who stole the show. They had some sort of secret rivalry between them that I could never figure out.

Now, Lucy M. was the craziest whack of a lesbian I ever laid eyes on. She worked for the National League of Nurses as the social director. Perfect because she loved to dress up, decorate and organize festivities. She may have been a fag in her past life, but I wasn't sure. Lucy had thick, neatly cropped, curly dark hair that she was always trying to control with some new hair product from a high-dollar beauty salon to Rite-Aid. Her bathroom was a beauty magazine's fantasy advertisement. She was tall and plump, but sultry through the masses of makeup and hairspray. She and Alma had been friends ever since Alma tried to pick her up at a party after too many margaritas. Lucy took her home, painted her toes and Alma threw up on her leopard skin carpet. After Lucy vomited, trying to clean it up, she shook hands with her and said let's just be friends. Everyone loved the Luce. When she had enough bourbon, she would pull out her baton while donning some gold sequined outfit she wore as a majorette in high school. Even though she was heavyset, the pinnacle of her routine would be the splits in the middle of the floor. Partyers would cheer, and Alma would always pull her up. Alma was good at pulling people up.

Anyway, Lucy and Alma and me were tight as ticks and our triangle was galvanized by the sheer irony of how different we all were from each other. Our only commonality was our proclivity for women. That was it. Otherwise, you could have seen all of us walking down the street at separate times of the day and would have seen a diesel flannel dyke—me; a plain Jane, two-dimensional skinny-ass bumbler—Alma; and a lesbian in a fag's body, long painted fingernails, Jewish batonist—Lucy.

"What was in the notes?" Lucy asked me then reached for the ketchup.

"No one ever found out. Elsie had been passing them back and forth for some time, though. Pass me the salt," I said. Our corner booth was the spot for rumor-central. Freddy's Corner Cafe in the heart of Carytown had made us our burgers and libations as long as we were old enough. It was a large joint with a faux mahogany bartop that meandered like a U-turn from the booths to the dance floor. Pool tables and foosball backed up to the end of the bar, and on weekends, live music played in front of the main bay windows. It was the kind of joint where homos gathered to eat home cooked diner food during the day, then came in late at night and on weekends to cruise chicks and dance and act cool. We rarely made it on weekends. The coolness had long ago eked out of our bodies.

"They hired a replacement for ol' Elsie," I said. "Some new girl from another Richmond high school."

Lucy looked at me with the look she always gave me when there might be a potential woman for me lurking somewhere—one eyebrow up, lips puckered. "Have you seen her?" she inquired. "Is she cute? She's a PE teacher and you know, Vera, five out of ten PE teachers reserve a spot on our committee? Do you think she may have homo-gymnotica, Ver?"

Alma looked quizzical.

Lucy rolled her eyes at her. "Dorcus Aramus. It means does she have the qualities we seek in a lesbo lover?" Lucy sipped her margarita.

"Now what might that be?" I asked.

Lucy swallowed. "Short haircut but not too butch. A body like Cindy Crawford but a face like Rossellini. Humor like Ellen and a smile like Jodie Foster, but not her personality."

Stung, Alma interrupted. "What's wrong with Jodie's personality. I think she's all right!" Lucy and Alma started their usual Mexican standoff. Lucy swirled her drink while I looked over at Elsie tending bar. She caught my eye and winked. I looked away.

"She directed that movie, *Home for the Holidays*. Lucy, good grief, did you see it?" Alma looked at her then looked at me for a commitment. I looked out the door to see if someone, who knows who, might arrive and get me out of the silly debate.

"Oh, Alma," Lucy signaled for another drink, "you know I can't stand her. She's a stuck-up snit who should have come out a long time ago. Plus her cheeks could be an ad for Hoover freakin' vacuums and that nose could cut a whole watermelon in half. That movie was way too namby-pamby for me, Al."

Alma slapped the ketchup bottle. "It's not namby-pamby. You just don't appreciate art."

"Well?" said Lucy looking at me.

"Well what?" I said. Lucy had a knack for making you feel uncomfortable even about things you didn't know you were supposed to feel uncomfortable about. Once she got a police officer so upset over why he wasn't out getting the real criminals that he just let her go after she had run a red light. Lucy's an awful driver. She could make even the most confident person squirm. I wasn't confident. I wasn't, really. And she was always pressuring me to feel and do things I wasn't supposed to.

"Is she cute?" came the retort. I sat and thought for a second. Her debut on the faculty had been a quiet one, however, I had seen her hanging around all the PE teachers and their unbreakable circle of secrecy and bondage. All flocking around one another as if they were a gaggle of fraternity brothers, smacking high-fives and spouting the most recent sports jive. I couldn't make sense of any of it. Why someone slaps you when you've done something good is beyond my scope and comprehension. "Good job" and an A-minus usually made me feel all right.

Anyway, I had seen her around the old PE piranhas. She was tall, about five-ten with dark hair. We'd bumped into one another in the office while reaching into our mailboxes. Curran was side by side with Bourdon. It was the way it laid itself out. I was reaching into mine and accidentally backed right up into her like a Freudian-physical slip. She dropped a note. I picked it up and remembered being eye to eye with her breasts. It was the kind of detail Lucy was always looking for.

"I've only seen her in the mailroom," I said.

Alma looked up from her sandwich. "Why don't they call it a female room?" She laughed and Lucy and I just stared at her. "Well, I thought it was kind of funny."

"You're a knucklehead, Alma. Vera"—she turned to me—"does she have potential? You know you've had quite the dry spell." She looked at Alma, puckered her lips, swigged her margarita and they both ayed in agreement. My dry spell was going on over ten years. I'd say it was more like the Mojave Desert dry spell. I had had visions but no luck. No oasis for a long time. I was happy in my routine, and the last girl I had gone out with had been a Democratic liberal who had a bi-level haircut and a truck with about a million rainbow stickers plastered all over it. I was incognito everywhere we went if we were in the rainbow mobile. It lasted eight months. After the breakup, I decided to get electrolysis for the mustache I felt like I had grown. No women for me—not in ten years. My dyke damper was shut, and I liked it that way. My friends were constantly bothering me about meeting someone, even a leaky fire hydrant in the middle of a New York City summer would have done me good Lucy had said to me once.

"She's all right. But, you know I'm not a sports enthusiast, so we don't have much in common," I said.

Alma piped in through a fry. "Who cares about that. If she can carry on a conversation with you, and if she likes beer, well, Vera, you're halfway there." She pushed her glasses up with her middle finger.

"Dorcas—Shhh." Lucy stopped her. "Listen, who cares

about conversation and beer. If she's got sex appeal then you're really halfway there. I'm not going to sit here and say that looks don't matter, Veer. We need to get you guys hooked up at some sort of rendezvous as quickly as possible. Come on, Veer! It's the best situation, and you're not getting any younger!

"A meeting with our twenty questions to run by her." Lucy and Alma had a list. "We'll get Alma to write up her questionnaire, and then we can all pick a few and nonchalantly ask her a few questions each. Okay, I'll ask her about her past. Alma will ask her about her social skills, and you can ask her about her English background. If she passes, then we have to get her to do the hard part."

"What's that?" I interjected.

"Like you," Lucy said emphatically.

I squirmed around in my seat and fiddled with the back of my hair. I guess she was a dating possibility in the middle of my impossible life. I had seen her in the mailroom and on her jaunts by the library. She was beautiful in a handsome way. And Elsie had confirmed that she was on the homo committee with us, fresh out of a two-year relationship with a girl from Elsie's flag football team.

"What if I don't want to go out with her? I'm not ready to date any ol' P.-damn-E. teacher. It goes against my nature and my style," I said.

Alma crunched another fry. "Vera," she said between bites, "you don't have a thing to lose."

"Yeah, Veer. Nothing to lose"—Lucy looked at me then shrugged her shoulders—"plus, hon, I hate to tell you something, you have no style. Right, Alm?" Alma confirmed with a nod and another middle finger up her nose.

"What?" I spouted back.

"You don't have any style." Lucy cemented it and was right. I had no style, no taste, except for what to read on a cold winter's night.

We began the plan. Lucy told me that her friend Brock could fix my hair and that she could suave me up and lend me an outfit of hers. Elsie joined in from the bar and said she knew someone who could arrange an impromptu meeting at one of the gay educational advocacy meetings she knew Frankie Bourdon went to. Another one was coming up soon and I should go. Gay advocacy was not my cup of tea I told them. I was far into my own homophobic closet and liked it there. More rainbow flags and stickers and everyone saying it's time to shout it loud and clear—"We're HOMOS and we love it!"—made me want to throw up. No one in their right minds wanted to hear any of that. We'll be shot for sure.

How we would do this, I didn't know. Alma and Lucy were at the bow, me far back at the stern looking for a way to jump ship.

Two weeks later, Lucy had me over to paint my face at her house after we were ensured by a friend of a friend of Elsie's that the Bourdon girl would be there. I felt like an ass. I'd seen her floating around campus but no more mailroom visits. Now I was some kind of secret agent who had to get her face and outfit handled by the experts.

"What are the questions we're gonna ask?" Alma had a legal pad and sat atop Lucy's bed. Lucy milled around the room grabbing makeup and clothes and anything she thought might help the "look" that she was going to create for me.

Lucy made me shut my eyes and dangled a thick bone of dark mascara over them. "Number one. Are you dating anyone?"

Alma stopped her. "Elsie already told us she was single."

"Alma, Frankie doesn't know we know. Vera sit still. If you don't, I'm going to poke you in the eye." I stopped fiddling.

"Number two," Alma returned, "are you in any kind of psychotherapy at the present time? If so, how many times a week and what for?"

Then Lucy said, "Number three. When and how often do you like sex? Top or bottom or a switch?" Alma rolled her eyes.

"Number four," I chime in. "Do you think I hang around a bunch of nimrods? True or false, check the box."

"Lucy?" Alma asked. "What's a switch?" She pushed her glasses.

"Darlin', that's a person who can do both top and bottom, regardless." Lucy swathed on the blush then began penciling my lips.

"Oh!" Alma stopped. "What are you, Vera. Top, bottom or switch?"

"I'm a Republican," I said.

Lucy handed me a mirror and pulled the back of my hair. "You're on the bottom then. Republicans always lay back to get some good Democratic ass." Thirty minutes of poking, prodding and questioning and finally, "What do you think, Veer?"

I held the mirror up, the mascara massacre complete. I looked like Lucy's twin. I was lathered in black outlines on my upper and lower lids, and my face had some sort of brown hue to it. "I look like a painted midget at a clown show for lesbian fags. Do you need to blow dry any of this to my face so it'll stick to my facial hair. Good God, Lucy! I look like a caricature of . . . well . . . you!"

"What's wrong with that?" Lucy looked at Alma. Alma looked at the both of us and said she thought it was fine and let's get back to the questions.

"Number five. Would you go out with a Lucy McGillicutty look-a-like except without the baton and Jew nature and sexual expertise?" I located a towel and wiped it off.

"What did you do that for?" Lucy barked.

"Lucy?" I asked. She waited. "I really think it should just be you and me and Alma tonight. You know, the three of us here in your house, your room. We've got you, a switch for sure. Alma, a bottom for sure, and me—"

"What? What are you Vera?" Alma let her glasses slip.

"I'm nervous," I admitted.

"Shut up, Vera. You'll be fine. Alma?" Lucy scuttled over to her friend and put her arm around her.

"Yeah?"

"Vera's queerer than I thought."

We rolled to Freddy's for the beer prequel to drink up prior to my debut at the advocacy meeting. I was being tortured, but, that was all right. I was with my buds and as screwed up as they were—top, bottom, switch, whatever—I still had a liking for them.

Chapter 2

Twice a year, what I called the pink triangle organization for teachers held a meeting to discuss the latest trends on the homosexual waterfront. It was very political, if you ask me. I had found it kind of hilarious that they all gathered together in their own separatist group talking about inclusiveness. Lucy and Alma went because of their Democratic propensities and because wherever one goes the other followed. Alma, being an educator, felt the "call." Lucy, the partier, loved the drinks. Everyone gathered together in separate factions to talk about fighting together—girls on one side, boys on the other. I rolled my eyes at the irony of the situation.

By the fireplace, I found my nook as the party's wallflower, and my eyes rotated like a periscope from the fags on one side twitting over one another to the Joes (my name for lesbians or dykes) on the other side, hunkered down to watch football. Clothes, leather and sex from one end, scores, high-fives and chips on the other. Politics waited till halftime. Bi-level haircuts from the Eighties were still in style. My mongoloid-bowl cut had been in and out of style three times since I began wearing it. A familiar emptiness filled my void of a body, and I felt like Holden Caulfield.

In the first chapter of *The Catcher in the Rye*, ol' Holden was feeling mighty sorry for himself because he forgot the equipment for the fencing team on their way to this huge tournament in New York City. Holden was the manager and held responsible for losing the equipment and, ultimately, responsible for the defeat by forfeiture. Then he went back to Pencey Prep and dropped out because of that and the fact that he was failing miserably because it was Christmas, and he missed his dead brother. On the other hand, I did not feel sorry for anyone in this place. It was the Holden as outcast/Vera as outcast that had enveloped my self consciousness. Conversations about makeup and flower arrangements or sports statistics and Ford pickups vexed and puzzled me. For a second, I was sickened by the omnipotent stereotypes that had swarmed the room of this pink triangle affair and its pretentious blah, blah, blah. I pulled my white turtleneck down over my swollen Buddha belly and noticed there was a twittish one from across the room glancing my way. I wondered if he thought I was a man. It sometimes happened. Nonchalantly, I turned to the mirror and covertly check for any white bats hanging in the cave. There I was. I saw what they all must have seen but didn't really care. Scarred skin from teenage acne stretched over my face where the bleached peach fuzz looked extra impressive in the sunlight from the window. A neolithic beetle brow, the precipice that shaded my lower lids, my canyons of dark doom. I understood why Gracie was my sole companion. I looked away—the cave was clear. That's all I really cared about. Holden, I thought, you really screwed it up yourself. Who cares about your dead brother. It was just a stupid book anyway. And this meeting was stupid.

I looked to Alma and Lucy who had been chatting it up with the Joes about short fingernails and presidential hopefuls and who was doing the Bahamian all-women's cruise. I mouthed to them that I wanted to go, but my pleading went unnoticed, so I picked up the Walt Whitman reader and read a poem about a lonely tree in Louisiana. It couldn't have gotten any worse. It was me. I was the tree. I was on the open road and before you knew it, I was in the land of myself, the song of myself, on the open road with my Sketchers on. I ran by the bears, trapped the wolves, lit up the sky with fireworks from the air I breathed out.

A cheeseball zoomed by my face. I looked up. My eyes were out of focus from my own transcendent mysticism I'd sugared myself with. Lucy stared at a hole in my chest. I looked down to see if there was any smoke. None. I looked back at Luce. Her head went back and forth like she had the dancing palsy just like when my nephew danced. Alma gave me her noted glasses push and started doing the same thing. They were the palsy sisters, I thought. Almost uncontrollably, I began to do it with them. Bounce-a, bounce-a, bounce-a. It was then that I realized burgeoning from my poetry coma that they were practically head-butting each other over the woman who was standing behind me—Frankie Bourdon. While in my Whitman trance, she must have slipped in. Just then I felt sorry that I bucked ol' Holden. I felt that I wanted to be Holden Caulfield on the bus to New York to find himself. I looked around for a cup of courage, a pint of self-esteem, a pair of tweezers. Nothing in sight.

Then, the worst thing imaginable happened. I pooted. Lucy was now going to her death for making her "death" chili the night before. I had tried not to, but in my nervousness, it squeaked out. A pop, really. I grasped at the bottom of my shirt. A few people looked my way as I did the obligatory cover-up to the poot—I coughed. Frankie and the woman she was talking to stopped to look at me. The dreaded fart had come out of the closet, and I stood there holding the door. Time stood still.

Anxiety is always mitigated with a cigarette. I rifled to my pocket, pulled one out, and lit it as fast as the wind I had just broken. The palsy sisters now palsied it even worse. I knew what they were thinking—"Don't smoke!" Then, I realized that my agility at getting it lit was too slow. The funky green orb arrived. Frankie and her company shuffled away. I stood there—farty and funky, funky and farty. Whitman's poetry, which had been tucked underneath my arm, slipped and, boom, smacked to the floor. I bent over to pick it up, but before I could, a hand reached down and grabbed it, a strong, veiny, muscular hand with olive skin. With my head still down near my own green dungeon of death, I blurted out "thanks!" and then, on my way up, found myself eye to eye with a barrel of cleavage. The mailroom debutante struck again.

She handed me the book. "What are you reading?" came the husky voice, but she answered her own question before I could say anything. "Oh, I see. Walt Whitman," she pulled the book back and looked at the title. "Any good poems?"

I fervently glanced to Alma and Lucy. Their eyes were riveted, and Alma was holding on to Lucy's elbow. I managed to look at Frankie. I managed to talk, although the panic put me into my double-vortexed tunnel where my eyes acted like double lenses, my dry mouth blubbered out words in a cotton brain. Two camera lenses my eyes became, one back in my brain fumbled through the silvery threads to words—subjects, verbs, objects. The other lens looked at the object to which I must be talking but not hearing or believing a sound I made.

"Uh, why, yes"—I reached for the book—"I was just reading one about a tree in Louisiana." I fumbled to find it. "It's right here on page twenty-three."

She moved closer. "Must have been some tree for someone to write a poem about it," she said.

"Yes, some tree it is. Here, do you want to read it?" Lucy and Alma were now Siamese twins four feet away looking through the blinds and jabbering over what-I-don't-know. I pulled my shirt and scratched my cheek. I hesitated and looked back at this Frankie girl.

"No, that's okay. I'm not a poetry lover," she smiled. "Hey, aren't you the librarian at my school? I don't believe we've met. I'm Frankie Bourdon, the new PE teacher. I took over for Elsie Miser just this past month." She put out her hand. I was almost too ashamed to shake it. My fingernails were down to the quick and the sweaty palms were no help. But I did.

"It's nice to meet you. I'm Vera Curran, the librarian. I shelve books anywhere from the two hundreds to the nines," I said this then regretted it because I puzzled her. Perhaps she didn't understand librarian-ese.

"Nice to meet you. Hey, Paulie, wait—" And then she was gone.

The Siamese cavalry arrived as I snuffed out my cigarette. Holden would have turned his hunting cap around backward and gone out into the stillness of the night toward the train tracks. Not me. I felt misread, unbundled and ready to go. Lucy put her arm around me and bumped me with her hip.

"Wow, Veer. That turbo shock really did wonders for your sex appeal. We thought we were going to have to evacuate. That fart registered high on the sphincterometer." She laughed and so did Alma.

Alma bumped the other side, "Yeah, Vera, the psycho survey is going to have to wait now since you can't do the cheek clinch well enough. Hey, Lucy, we're going to have to practice walking around with metal bars in our buns or something." They were so funny. I pulled my shirt over my Buddha belly and bumped them both back.

"Let's go back to Freddy's," I said. "At least I can be myself with you two nimrods and don't have to worry about my face and my body and my flatulence. The lights are low and the music is too loud." I walked out the door.

Once in the car, I got the grilling from the once Siamesers now turned CIA agents.

"What happened? What did she say?" Lucy put on some lipstick and checked me from the rearview mirror while Alma fumbled with the heat and radio. We roared down Oakmont and headed to Monument Ave. Alma found Bruce and the volume went up. All of us smelled like beer and cigarettes.

"We passed cordial notes," I said. "That was all."

"Like Elsie passed to her student?" Alma inquired sarcastically.

"Forget Freddy's," I said. "Just take me home." I was now the new poster child for embarrassment. "I can't believe I did that."

Alma turned around. "Oh, come on, Vera! You were fine. It happens to the best of us. Even the President farts."

"The First Lady does, too," Lucy interjected. "And, I bet Jodie Foster does and Susan Sontag and Sarah Schulman and Katie Couric and Matt Lauer and the biggie of them all."

"Who?" Alma and I say in unison.

"Vladimir Putin. Who's pootin? Is Vlad Putin pootin?" She laughed so hard at her own joke that we nearly ran off the road and hit a stop sign.

Levity. The one thing Luce was good at. My face burned, though. I wanted to go to bed with a container of Cool Whip and a box of Oreos. When they left me at the steps to my house in Louisa, I walked away and gave them a wave in the air without looking back. I read and slumbered and thought about the Bourdon girl and my embarrassment. How would I even face her on Monday? She didn't even talk to me for a second. I would avoid her. Space and time, time and space. That would settle it all down. I'll feel better by the year 2050, I'm sure.

"Stop!" Kyle let Gracie out of the back door.

"What?" I said.

"You mean the first real conversation you have with Frankie, it was two lines about a tree in Louisiana and gaseous? Aunt Vera, that's not very thrilling or romantic. My professor is going to laugh me out of psychology two-o-one." He went back to the kitchen through my double doors where he continued to converse while making a sandwich.

We were on my deck, and I reached for a cigarette and looked out at the sky. Gracie-Mac dug a hole by an old pine tree that stood nearly ninety feet high. Always the digger. Squirrels would run up the tree, and she would bark her head off and then dig as fast as she could like it was a way of covertly catching the squirrel. Weird dog.

"Where do you want me to start then?" I asked. I could hear the fridge door open and shut. I inhaled harder and thought further back. Kyle returned. Turkey on rye with mayo, his favorite.

"How about an anecdote from your childhood that is interesting that I could tell the class. Coming out or whatever. Something to color it." He swigged another beer and looked at me.

I looked at my mantel above the fireplace where a picture of

Alfred Lord Leighton's "Flaming June" spectacularly lit up my wall. I took another drag from my cigarette and thought.

This is what I told him:

Perhaps it really got started when I was a small child of about seven. My dad was drunk from the vodka and momma was taking Valium in the back of our big, yellow mobile home. Across the mountain highway was a ridge. No one noticed that I walked across the road and climbed it. I looked up the side of the hill and then back at the camper. I stood still, almost cataleptic, among purple and yellow wildflowers in a blue-striped shirt with gold shorts and green tennis shoes somewhere between the Grand Canyon and eternity. Over and over again, I watched the wind sway the flowers. The sky's clouds, cotton and virgin white, sailed over my head going to the in-between place I couldn't think of. I just stood there and looked. I was only seven years old, and I told myself to remember this moment for all time and that someday I would need to go back there, here to this place, to my youth, for a place to remember, a strange home.

I didn't know what the word dysfunctional meant because it was the seventies and people weren't reading all of those self-help books yet. So, I stood there in those wildflowers just a staring away at everything around me. It was beyond me what I would become or what the stars had already written for me. If you asked me, it's pretty screwed up. I mean just standing there as a seven-year-old staring at a bunch of wildflowers already feeling like no one understood me. I am pretty damned messed up with my sexuality because of what happens in between my legs when I looked at my momma's *Cosmopolitan* magazine. What did it mean? My heart beat harder and my knees tingled from all the pretty pictures. I hid away in the bathroom with them in the camper. It was the only peace anyone got while you were in some camper for six week trying to have a family vacation and everyone was either drunk or having a nervous breakdown.

I was a year younger than my brother, and most of the time in those days he pretended I was a Klingon. Older sister Katie sang Elton John's "Island Girl" into her hairbrush while we drove down the road. She was already thirty even though she was thirteen. Playing Captain Kirk instead of a Klingon was my outlet as I saved the pretty women. I used the throw pillow from the tiny couch and pretended it was the head of the girl I'd just saved from my brother Jack and the Klingons and kissed her like I was Captain Kirk. She kissed me back. I smiled at her, assured she wants to kiss me more. Sometimes I got real passionate and laid down with the pillow and kissed her a lot. My legs trembled and my stomach dropped to my feet. I made dead sure no one was watching—dead sure. It was a big secret to keep, kissing people and acting like you're Captain Kirk.

That's probably when my homo behavior started.

Keeping secrets is a tricky thing.

Years later, I continued to tell Kyle, the secret became even trickier.

Late October at Louisa High School was notable by its Norman Rockwellian landscape and people. Originally, the school was built as a series of outbuildings that were attached by a labyrinth of concrete walkways and overhead canopies to keep away rain and snow. Later, one large building with a hallway was added to make it look more like a high school. The brilliance of the landscaping and flowers kept up by the custodians made the greenery come alive with brown and green and red colors even if the buildings themselves were over sixty years old. Almost overnight, the maple trees gave birth to yellow and orange that would make any Vermonter cringe with jealousy. It was an unknown tract of rural Americana—a place that had been my home for nearly twenty years. Three days a week, I ate there. Large baked rolls, turkey and mashed potatoes and fudgies were served every Monday. Thursday would be Monday's rolls with spaghetti and Friday was always pizza and french fries. The football team consistently lost half or more of its games, and the student body hardly paid any attention to the faculty who were themselves ready to be permanently placed in a picture inside the glass cases in the main office. The football field stood next to the tennis courts and the baseball and softball fields were hidden by a small hill beyond them. The student parking lot intimated what most parents did for a living. Old pickups meant stone warehouse or mechanical job. Chevettes were usually divorced mothers who worked in one of the two cafes in town. Camaros were plumbing and electricity. Sedans, 1985 or later, were church workers or a pastor. Bicycles were the vehicles of those on welfare because dad was a drunk and mom couldn't get a call into social services.

When I got to school on Monday, I walked by the flagpole like I always did and saw the same kids hand-in-hand in prayer. I hoped they prayed for me since I was on my way into the mailroom, a place where I'd seen the Bourdon girl. I saw Maggie Winterfield, head varsity cheerleader, her boyfriend Holt Meyers, the captain of the wrestling team; Marty Hanna, the lead in that year's play, *Romeo and Juliet*, and his following of choristers of six or seven freshmen girls, plus the head-prayer-leader-in-charge. On this particular day, however, there was an exception. The "he" had been replaced by a "she," whom I didn't know. I wouldn't have cared much about this person except for one glaring detail—the loudest, brightest, reddest hair since Bozo the Clown. Tammy Faye Bakker's sister and her spider-lash lids that must have been glued on in the late 1800s. Twinses for sure. Her glasses hung about her tired, wrinkled neck, a green striped suit and freshly polished black pumps. But the hair! My gawd! A beacon, a firetruck—Gracie would howl. I looked for orange cones that might say: "Lookout! Do a U-turn before it's too late."

Then in a circle, with clasped outstretched hands, they recited the cadence of the Lord's Prayer. At the end, each lifted their head and I caught her, the striped one's, eye. I looked down quickly as a pack of wild geese flew overhead in winged attention. Then I heard Carol Anderson, my cohort in crime in the library, call after me.

"Hey, Vera! How was your weekend?" she asked as we walked into the office, which was also the repository for the dreaded mailroom. I managed to converse in the average discourse of "fine" and "yours" and sucked in my Buddha belly hoping the worst wouldn't happen.

It did. I couldn't believe it actually did.

A voice from behind called out. "Hey, you! Yo! You packing 'em in the nine-hundreds today?" Fear expunged to reality.

"Oh, Ms. Bourdon!" The Green Lantern more like it. She wore a squishy green PE suit, and her eyes lit up in the same color. She towered over me and immediately her aura, her enigmatic energy was felt. Stunned for a second, I then blurted out, "Why yes, I am shelving in the nines today." Carol passed me, unobservant to the quandary I was in, and headed into the library, just across the hall from main office.

Side by side in the mailroom, we continued our conversation.

"So what do you shelve in the nine hundreds?" She pulled her mail out and rifled through it. The question was a nonchalant nicety she threw out without looking at me.

I mimicked her mail sorting and responded. "History, religion, that sort of thing. I don't spend much time jamming them in there. Usually, I'm in the nine-hundreds packing away the more interesting ones like drugs, sex, alcoholism and teen pregnancy."

"Heck, that's not as bad as the six-hundreds." She looked at me and could tell by the quizzical look that took shape on my face that I was lost by the comment. Then she looked through the window. "See that lady out there?" She pointed. I looked to see Bozo the Clown incarnate who I'd passed on the way in.

"Yes," I said. She pulled an apple from her pocket and quickly bit into it. The juice dripped down the side of her mouth, and she wiped it fervently with the back of her hand.

"That lady, Ms. Librarian, is in the six hundred sixty-sixes! Shhhhh"—she put her index finger to her lips—"but, don't tell anyone."

"What? I'm confused. Why is she in the six hundred sixty-sixes, and why can't I tell anyone?" I pulled my shirt down and clenched my buttocks.

"Because, her and I share the same genes."

"You mean *she*," I corrected. "And what do you mean jeans?"

For a moment, she was paralyzed. Time floated through the cerebral air. And then, I realized my blunder. I had corrected her grammar.

"Don't tell me," she went on, "her taught you English?"

My face went down in search of an apology on the carpet. "Sorry, I didn't mean to correct your grammar . . ." I tried to look at her but to no avail. The cells below the surface of my skin spread the red fire of embarrassment across my neck and face like dark ink.

"That's okay, librarian in the nine-hundreds. I won't correct your body for any of its idiot-syncrasies." She winked and then said, "Nice word, eh?"

Frankie Bourdon turned and began her morning journey to the gym, squishy green gym outfit and all. I wasn't sure if I even liked the girl up until then. I had just tagged along with my cavalry comprised of Alma and Lucy. However, the long, dark one had for the first time truly caught my attention. She was quick and witty, I thought, not something you often see in PE teachers. Old Elsie was bright but had been stupid in the note writing department with that player of hers. I wondered if Frankie knew of the repercussions if anyone found out about her own propensities for women. Virginia and school districts and the homo thing were cloaked in the bowels of the Bible and the right wing even if Jefferson had his bill for religious freedom. Pervasive Southern anger about families was entrenched and unforgiving, relentless and formidable. No one messed with it. Never.

Frankie must have fooled them with her looks—tall and thin and muscular, no question mark here about her body type. And her skin was olive and toned, no pores. Her facial symmetry was punctuated by a young schoolgirl's French roots—small nose, thin lips, high cheek bones, all contrasted by her large dark blue eyes that could probably steal the breath from any man or woman. Her hands—I saw them rifling through the mail—are even, muscular and thick with arching blue veins. She had outsmarted them with her wit, too, and had probably given our principal an erection. These were the three things that got new teachers hired at our school—looks, wit and a stiffie. If you ask me, those things got anyone anywhere hired.

She had winked at me. My day went by as if I were the air in my own sails. I blew here and there on my currents of sudden Bourdon happiness. T.S. Eliot and Gracie Mac were part of my ritual later that night. I fed her a rawhide. She chewed. I read. When we went to sleep, I looked out my window and saw stars. Like an old David Cassidy record, I replayed our conversation and the winking over and over again in my mind. My stomach dropped like Captain Kirk's did a long time ago. A voluminous half-surreal voice played on my mind's record player. "Shhhhh"—a finger to parted lips—"but don't tell anyone."

I won't, Frankie Bourdon. I won't.

Chapter 3

The next day, I decided to leave Frankie a note in her mailbox. Gracie-Mac signaled with a body wag over breakfast between the two of us that it would be okay. After two million crazy thoughts on what to say, I finally decided to give her an appropriate message. I found a Post-it note in the office on my way to the library and scribbled it out. "What do women do?" Philosophy 101. I signed it, "Packin' 'em in the 666s." I stuffed it quickly in her mailbox and banged my toe then tripped halfway into the library. I saw our Napoleonic principal, Mr. Dixon, with his coke bottle glasses and pock-marked face. He sneered at me and then laughed. I jumped and made it in just as the late bell rang.

The day went by like all others. Classes came in and the teachers turned them loose on Carol and me. We ran around, proverbial chickens within the masses of Goths, the wannabe Goths, dreadlocks, posers posin', sags a bustin', flipping fingers. "Shhh! Be quiet," I said, "two to a table." We checked them in and checked them out. I smoked four cigarettes for lunch out back at Fort Apache. We named it that when the school custodians built a six-foot-high wooden wall around the back of Building Nine. There was a picnic table inside of it littered with ashtrays and empty Coke cans. The smoke signals poured out. I cruised through fifth, sixth and seventh periods, checked my mailbox for Post-it notes from the gym—nothing. At three, just thirty minutes before the close of the day, one of the flagpole prayees came into the library. He found me underneath a table plugging a computer back into its printer.

"Miss Curran?" a voice called. The "miss" was a distinctive *mith.*

"Yes." I crawled out. "Hey, Holt! How are you? How was your wrestling match last night?" I finished plugging in the printer.

"Great! I p-p-pinned him in just under two m-m-minutes." Holt was the best senior wrestler for heavyweights in the district. He was six-two and easily a hundred and ninety-five. He wasn't heavy. His lisp was his only weakness, which he tried to hide by stuttering. In elementary school, the children had slaughtered him with lisping mockeries. He turned to weight lifting and most of them shut up, at least to his face. The girls loved him because he was soft-spoken, muscular and thick. Most days he spent in the library pretending to read sports magazines and looking for his girlfriend.

"Uh, Miss Curran. Do you have a s-s-second, *ahem*?" he whispered and looked around.

"Sure." I stood up next to him and looked around too. "See anyone you know?" I mocked him.

"I'm doing a- a- a report for my h-h-history class on the influences of religion on s-s-s-social thinking, and there is a small problem." He sputtered out the last part and looked around again. He leaned in. "Can we go in your offce?" I obliged and we did.

"What is it?" I closed the door and leaned into him.

"The teacher is a-a-asking that my group look at the ones in the Bible that talk about s-s-s-sodomy, and stuff like that." He looked through my office window into the library. His girlfriend Maggie was walking in. She stopped by a group to chat. Uncomfortable already in my shoes, he turned to me and then, a pregnant pause.

I squirmed a bit and said, "Is he asking you what I think he's asking you?"

"Y-y-y-yes, and my group appointed me to be the s-s-s-spokesperson. None of them wanted to do it and it's a huge project grade for the marking period."

"Whatever happened to don't ask, don't tell? Or separation of church and state?" I sat down and picked up a pad of Post-its and doodled while we talked.

Holt sat down. "E-e-exactly what I thought. But he s-s-said that for a s-s-study of hate groups that we all wanted to study, like the k-k-k-KKK or whatever that we had to research the r-r-r-reathon why they hated and what groups they hated. He said that we needed to include at least three minorities in our presentation and one of our g-g-guys said the homosexuals would be a g-g-g-good one. He hates them like that Rocker guy in Atlanta. You know, the b-b-baseball player." I nodded. "Now we have to figure out the root cause of the hatred. For them, much of it is in the Bible. But no one in my group w-w-wants to come to the library to find the s-s-stuff. They are too embarrassed to be asking questions." He stopped.

In all of the years as either a teacher or librarian, no one had ever asked me a thing about homosexuality. Not once had I ever even remotely discussed it with anyone. I didn't even talk about it with half the people I knew. I hesitated there with Holt and stared down at the Post-it. Philosophy 101.

Finally, I said, "Why don't you all pick something else to do? When is it due? Maybe you can do an alternative assignment. No pun intended. Holt"—he spotted his girlfriend Maggie and switched his gaze from me to her, back and forth—"it's an uncomfortable topic for a lot of people, including me."

Holt talked faster. Maggie came our way. "We already a-a-asked him, and he s-s-said it was too late. We're past the deadline to change it." Holt looked desperate. I looked guilty. What in the world was I going to do?

At the door, Maggie stood in her cheerleader uniform. Her blond hair was thick and cut short to her head. Epitome of cute cheerleader, cute boyfriend. Her mother was on the school board, and her father, who had played football for the University of Richmond, was a well-known Baptist preacher in the community. The two, Maggie and Holt, were inseparable. When she walked in, Holt's face lit up. Puke.

"Hey, Miss Curran. Hey, Holt. What are you all up to?" She slid her backpack to the floor.

I looked at Holt who lost the words. I found them. "We were just talking about Holt's history project, Maggie. What are you up to?"

"Oh, nothing. I just popped in to grab a newspaper. My dad's in it again. Something about the new controversy about the AIDS hospice they're trying to put up in someone's neighborhood. My dad's on the board and is getting help from Mrs. Bourdon. It's crazy. Everyone's up in arms." She slid her arm into Holt's.

I couldn't believe it—two homo topics in two minutes. A bag over my head was what I needed. "Do you mean Ms. Bourdon, the new gym teacher is helping your dad? You're kidding?" I inquired.

"No, Miss Curran. I think it's her mom, though. She's our new prayer leader and works on the mission board with my dad." She turned to Holt, "Can you give me a ride home after gymnastics? Mom's at her league meeting and Dad's in Richmond at St. Mary's caring for some dying guy in ICU."

"Not a p-p-p-problem," Holt sputtered out. "Miss Curran, do you th-th-think you can help me anyway?" He was speaking about his topic. Being the head looker-upper in charge, I submitted to the torture. Why me? The deep-in-the-closet librarian.

I paused, then nodded in agreement. "Why don't you come by tomorrow. I'll do some research for you and see what we can come up with." I winked at Maggie. She smiled, and they left. On the way out, Holt, lisp and all, told me that I was the best.

I stood there looking at my doodled Post-it. The day was nearly over, and it crossed my mind that I needed to check my mailbox for any responses. Resigning myself to the fact that there would only be emptiness, I meandered aimlessly around the stack of books, picked up dried-up spitballs, pushed in chairs and rearranged some tables. Two boys sat in the corner looking at magazines. I watched them snicker over what I didn't know nor care. Suddenly, I found myself in the middle of a conversation that Lucy and Alma and I had had about sexual prowess and the naming conventions for said actions. We were all at Freddy's one Sunday for brunch, and Lucy was discussing how she used to hate to give hand jobs or blow jobs when she was in high school.

"They were so disgusting. But, mainly the blow jobs.

You never knew when the stack was to blow then you were hanging—swallow, retract completely or spit the stuff on the sheets." She wriggled in her seat.

"Why do they call it a blow job? I mean do we have something like that for women? Is there a saying?" Alma looked at Lucy then at me.

I cocked my head to one side. "Now Alm. Look at me, goofy. Do you think I know what we should call it? Hell, I am not even sure if I remember how to do it."

Lucy smiled. "Oh, Vera. Remember the bike, babe. Just like riding a bike."

Alma chimed in. "Yeah, just like a bike, Veer."

"Alma, when's the last time you partook, young lady?" Lucy asked. We stared at her while she pushed the glasses up.

"Well, it wasn't eighty-three or ninety-three. I'm not as bad as Vera."

"Hey," I interrupted. "I'm no nineteen eighty-three."

"Who cares," Lucy countered, "when, Alma?"

"I don't know. Two years maybe. It was with that postal girl from Oklahoma."

"You mean Okla-*homo*." I laughed, and we all clinked our glasses.

Lucy pondered. "We should call the cunni thing something other than the clinical term. It needs its own name. Hmmm. How about 'clitting the collar' or 'licking the little man'?"

Alma laughed. "It sounds very gay male. 'Licking the little man'? Come on Lucy, we can do better than that! How about 'sucking the little spud'?"

I laughed. "Now we sound like an ad for a pornographic Wendy's." We stopped then Lucy shoved her hands in the air.

"I have it!"

"What?" Alma and I said it in unison.

"Sweeping the deck," she was thrilled at her words.

"No, no, no!" Alma stopped Lucy. "I have an even better one. Swabbing the deck."

All three of us stopped. Yes. Swabbing the deck. It was a clean clitty cipher. Who could decode it but us. We were thrilled. An epiphany. Lucy looked at Alma in amazement. Alma looked at her and winked, something I'd never seen her do.

After the momentary fantasy of our swabbing-the-deck group brunch was over, I giggled to myself and managed to rearrange some papers on my desk. Carol closed shop. I picked up a pad of Post-its, and I wrote a note to myself.

What do women do? I wrote, then answered—*Women dream.*

"Stop! Aunt Vera? Don't tell me this. It started with a Post-it note? That's inconceivable, the craziest thing I've ever heard!" Kyle scribbled something on his notepad and cut off the recorder while Gracie-Mac curled up beside him.

I looked out my bay window to a stretch of my front yard. The maple tree under where Frankie and I had once stood looked more bent than usual. For a moment, everything seemed to merge from yellow to orange. The greenery and pale blue sky acquiesced into each other at the horizon's line as a gaggle of birds, suddenly and without notice, darted out from beneath a nestle of overgrown forsythia. Eileen Bourdon flashed into me. I stared momentarily at her then dismissed it like a bad dream. Panting, Gracie-Mac nudged me with her nose. I need to go out, she said.

"Why don't we go out for a minute, Kyle, and take a break." I lifted myself from the couch feeling slightly dismantled. "Come on, Gracie-Mac, go get your ball." *Shwoomp.* Two seconds later, there was a frenzy of the ball, drool-dom and a tail as lethal as a corked baseball bat. Grace the shadow—in the day, the night and times in between. Tufts of white gray around her mouth gave her age away, however, her demeanor was a Lab still possessed by fetching. "Get dat ball, girl," I would yell.

On his third beer, Kyle agreed. Fresh air was a good idea. "Do you want a beer, Aunt Vera?"

"Oh, why not. Sure, bring me one." He jumped up, rocketed to the fridge and grabbed two cold ones. We clinked them together outside.

"Are you doing okay?" Kyle asked. Our gait was slow as we crossed my yard. He put his arm around my shoulder. I put my hand on his hand.

"I was till I saw that," I said.

"What?" He turned to where I pointed.

From the bottom of my hill, I could hear the rickety motor of the Oldsmobile paleolithic relic—an engine and four wheels. It caught a wheel coming around the bend that forked with my road and the main highway. Inside was the creation that created me, my mother, the monster. A shiver went up then down—the hair on my neck stood up in the anticipation of the fires that might ignite. The last time she had come, we had fought over how to iron a simple cotton shirt. "No, not that way, Vera. What's wrong with you?" She would look at me with pursed lips. "Where did you get this shirt anyway? Don't you make any more money now since you got your master's or are you still in debt?"

My en garde was tattered. The thing with mothers was really more than I could bear. The last twelve months had been the hardest of my life. My crusade had changed, and Momma was pissed. Her mission in life was to continue her misery by exacerbating mine. Misery Ministries—her biggest success. I was not alone. It was the only thing my brother and sister and I had in common. We could do no good. It was worse for me, though. Jack and Katie had both money and style. I had a mongo haircut and had to get my beard waxed twice a month. It was the only beauty management I did besides buy aloe vera lotion from Target when it was on sale.

She punched between the brakes and the accelerator and came up my driveway like a wounded Oldsmobile in heat. The car had seen her wrath, too. I felt sorry for it.

"Got your Wonder Woman bracelets on, Aunt Vera?" Kyle swigged his beer and got into a karate stance.

"Got 'em," I barked back. "I'll wait here while you get the invisible airplane. It's parked out back. If we fly out of here now, we can be in Key West in two hours and be sipping on margaritas." He laughed, playfully karate chopped Gracie-Mac then me. *Hiya.*

"To Key West and beyond!!!" *Hiya*, again. "Give me all your money, Aunt Vera!" *Hiya*. "Gracie-Mac, give me all your paws!" She managed two.

"Okay, buzzed light year! Go help her out of the car."

Key West with Kyle would be fabulous I thought. I had been to Fantasy Fest with Frankie, Alma, Lucy and old Elsie to watch the Women's Flag Football National Championships. Elsie got MVP for her role as best defensive back and every dyke in the city stayed drunk for forty-eight hours straight. Ha. Forty-eight hours straight. Like that would ever happen. I cracked myself up. Lucy had headed up the impromptu parade committee to make a float for our cause and—

"Veraaaaa!" Here came my mom—Sylvia Curran with her newly dyed gray-blue beehive. "What are you doing with this boy?" She pointed to him then pointed to me. I looked at the beer to which she was pointing. A pause, and then she said, "Have you all gone madhat around here?"

The world's best Mrs. Malaprop, my mom.

"Why, yes," I pointed out, "I've gone madhat. Kyle, you?" I took a swig.

He smiled. "I've got the maddest hat around. Hand me those grocery bags, Grandma, before you drop them." She obliged. "I'll run in and put 'em away."

Sylvia looked at me with a marginal look of contempt. "Don't eat the chocolate cake. It's for after dinner, not now." She looked at Kyle walking through the door as if he were a madcap madman. "Kyle, what's wrong with your hair? And, what's that hanging off your ear? Does your father know about it? Good grief, kids these days." Kyle ignored her. "No respect for their appearances, no respect for each other. Blowin' up school buildings and wearing trench coats and shooting each other out of the cradle. What are these kids coming to, Veer?"

I looked at a living, breathing rendition of an Easter egg in front of me. A caricature of herself—glasses with her initials on the outside, bulbous clip-on earrings, black polyester slacks with a flowered mock turtle neck that was too tight and black flats two sizes too small. Her ankles were swollen over the edges. She stood with one hand on her hip, the other hand holding a cigarette which, as always, needed flicking.

"Vera, are you listening to me?" she asked.

"Momma, when have I never listened to you?" I asked back.

"Well, if you need examples, then you might want to get your brain Cat scanned, cuz you have no memory either." She started up the walkway and Gracie-Mac jumped on her. "Go away, Grace. Go on now. I don't need an oversized lemon slobbering all over me. Do you have any chicken, Vera? I need to put on a casserole. I need some thyme. Do you have any butter? You know, you're always out of butter. Memory. Cat scan. That's what you need." She barked out the questions and nattered all the way through the front door.

I waited till she walked in and then under my breath said,

"The problem with kids these days is that their parents give them every goddamned thing they want. And, if you ask me, what they really need are a series of good ass-whippings. One good one for sassing their parents, one good one for sassing their teachers and two good ones for repeating the first two. After that, they should be told to work at McDonald's from eight to five every day, then go to a night job where they work in sweatshops till they get their act straight. After that, they can come back. We'll see if they want to sass anymore. Every kid should wear a uniform to school—white shirt, khaki pants, sneakers. I could be the model, the prototype. I've been wearing it to school for the last fifteen years. How does that sound? Sounds like a good idea to me. A few ass-whippings, a school uniform and if they act out, it's flipping burgs at Mickey D's." I needed another beer.

The man on Channel Five was flubbing out his boondoggle.

"These homosexuals need conversion before they take over the legitimacy of marriage, our schools, our children, our whole society. We have groups now in place in every major metropolitan city that are already underway in trying to get them to reform. But, your help is needed. With your support, we can help fund these groups with the necessities that will keep them in the local and national limelight. We need air time on local radio and TV stations. We need creative young people who will help create catchy advertising for their peers and who will spread the word of the Bible that this immoral way of life is a choice for people who are in bed with Satan himself. It is our mission to infiltrate localities across the nation, to educate our young people who are pressured by their peers to try this abominable lifestyle and to squelch all educational reform that insists on teaching AIDS education and that the homosexual lifestyle is okay. We need to get rid of liberal educational methods that promote the gay agenda and that demonize who we are—the Right-to-Lifers, the True Christian Coalition, Americans who believe in the scripture and the traditional way of life. Call us now and we can meet with you in your area in less than two days about how you can start this organization in your area and keep the mission going! The number to reach us is one-eight-hundred-no-homos. Call us now. Don't forget your child's future is at stake! We need to act now to promote our ideals, our goals on all levels—local, state and national."

I had a vision of Eileen Bourdon ironing her blouse for her morning prayer meeting, sipping her tea and then turning up the volume on her TV. Later, Frankie told me that Channel Five was her favorite.

I continued my story for Kyle:

Chapter 4

When I reached into my mailbox at school that Friday, there it was—my first Post-it note back. My eyes darted both ways, then I quickly looked down to its message:

What do women do? It was the first line.

Women? Why, women start movements at parties with libearian cohorts in crime. It was the second line. The third line said, *Meet me at Fort Apache on break.*

I reeled. It was my first date in ten years. I read it again to make sure. On my third reading, I nearly ran over Carol who was balancing a stack of books by the office door. I ran to my office and found a Post-it pad.

What do women do? The first line.

Send smoke signals. It was the second.

Practically leaping back into the office, I crammed it into

her mailbox. When I checked her schedule on the master list, I noticed that she might not get it in time. Then I made a daring move. I asked the principal's secretary if she would call for Frankie over the intercom and tell her to check her mailbox. She did. Minutes later, I saw Frankie walking the walkway that separated the main office from the library. I was super sleuthy, I thought. When she walked back by a few minutes later, she looked into the library's window. My stomach dropped. I giggled to myself.

Between third and fourth periods, an eternity drew itself out in hour-like minutes. I watched the clock and tried to think of what it would be that I would say to her. "Hey," I thought, "how you been?" or "Hey there, gym teach, how are the kids treating you?" or "Thanks for the note, want to go out with me?" or "How's your subject-verb agreement these days?" or "Swab your deck?" I was a goddamned idiot. That's what I was. An idiot savant. Oxymorons. Blah.

I arrived at Fort Apache after a run to the bathroom to check the nose hair for any bats. I was sad to see that we wouldn't be alone. Two teacher cronies, Dick Robinson from history, and Lyla Rose Washburn, English as a second language, already staked out spots. We exchanged hellos and all freakishly lit up cigarettes in almost the same manner.

Time was a precious commodity when you were a teacher and a smoker. These two were veteran teachers, veteran smokers and early-gravers. They graded papers with the butts of the cigarettes hanging precariously smart between their lips and red ink pens in between their fingers. As I waited, I noticed the sunken eyes, the cracked fingers tired from the toil of teaching and grading for more than fifty years of combined service. I sucked down my first smoke as I reviewed some homo information on the Bible for Holt. My head and hand formed a shadow over the contents so no one would see.

"Hey, libearian! Glad you could hook up!" I nearly rocketed from my seat. Frankie goddamned Bourdon came sauntering around the goddamned corner like she had been the chief of goddamned Fort Apache for a hundred years. "Boy do I need a smoke!"

"I didn't know you smoked. Doesn't this go against gym teacher morality?" She fumbled through her pockets then glanced at the cronies, no eye contact. She looked at me, and I just shrugged my shoulders. "Need a light?" The words came, finally.

"No, libearian, I need a tampax!" She said it out loud. I couldn't believe it. Like a stuck piglet, I squeaked. She smiled then said, "Got one? I'm out like the nineties." As she waited for me to rifle my pockets and bag, she plopped down right next to me. I handed her a Marlboro Red, and she quickly joked about how it was a kamikaze cigarette. My hands trembled as I lit it for her. She cupped her hands around mine as the flame married the tobacco, always like a first kiss. Robinson and Washburn continued the red scribblings as if nothing had happened. Jesus Christ, I thought. How could they not? As Frankie inhaled her first rush of filtered smoke, I watched her more this time than when I was in the mailroom. Her short and thick dark auburn hair was wet by her ears with sweat. The jawline, which managed to hold a droplet cascading from her ear, was square like her broad shoulders. The cheekbones on her face reminded me of Sophia Loren's, but it was her eyes that blew me clear above the smoke signals from Fort Apache. Even eyebrows with a natural arch framed the darkest, bluest eyes I, cliche or not, had ever laid eyes on. Resonant skin glowed from activity, and each time she raised her strong, veiny hands to inhale from the cigarette, I could barely stop myself from staring at them. I must be a hand girl, I thought. Handy. Hmm.

I watched her close her eyes on her second drag and said, "So, whatcha you been up to?" Yuck.

"Trying to get my health classes in the right seating arrangement. I tell you, I just need five or six more kids in my seventh period, and it'll make it an even forty. Let me break it down for you, libear. I really think we need to increase class sizes, cut teacher pay and let the Christian Coalition mandate what we should and should not teach in family life education. Oh, and also, let the administration keep on doing what they do best—believe what the kids say over what we say." Robinson and Washburn looked up, inhaled, caught her eye, then went back to their continued silence. I didn't know what to say. She was flat out matter-of-fact. So far, the first date was fairly successful. I searched in the silence for a moment.

It was then and only then that I recalled what I was reading the other night when Gracie-Mac and I were snuggled in my bed reading and chewing—I from T.S. Eliot, she from Pedigree. The "Four Quartets." I stumbled upon it looking for "J. Alfred Prufrock's Lovesong." In it, he talks of the great abstract concept of time and how it sometimes stops, totally stops. A still point. As if lycomodium powder sprinkled itself on the aspect of time, making it form in the air like a fingerprint. The still point was a moment of great wonder, great revelation, great meaning—all encapsulated in the far reaches of the mind, the heart, the soul. An apex of time that at a moment's recollection can be retrieved, recalled and retold in such detail that it emotes evocative in the one who describes and the one who listens—almost unfathomable, untouchable, unseeable, but, nevertheless there. Perhaps it was the proposal of marriage, or the winning of a scholarship or the first grandchild, or the vindication of a right that was once something done wrong. Eliot suggested that it is at this still point that the dance of life occurs. The dance of life,

I thought. I didn't know how to dance. Frankie had nice legs, now there's a still point.

"Yo, yo. Libear. Are you there?" With her question, my momentary trance-like state was lifted. "What are you thinkin' about?" I looked at her eyes, then down to my Buddha belly. I pulled my shirt down and lit another.

"Sorry. I travel to the distant yonder sometimes at a moment's notice when someone makes me think."

"And?" She looked at me. Her eyes scanned my body, I felt it. I sucked in on the inhale.

"Nothing. Maybe it was the line about teacher pay, class size and the Christian Coalition. It made me stop and think. I'm helping this kid out with his history project and the Bible and the root cause of hate group hatred has come up. Joy, joy, joy."

"I know plenty about that. My mom's a card carrying member. Spent half my life in between the right and the left. Joy, joy, joy." She mocked me.

I lit her final cigarette during the final moments of dream date number one. "Hey, thanks for the Post-it note back. How's it going for you here? Do you like Louisa High School?"

"Sure beats the hell out of the Navy," she smiled.

"You were in the Navy? How old are you, Bourdon?" Her eyes met mine, and I smiled at her. I was trying to flirt.

"How old do you think I am?" she inquired back, one eyebrow arched up over her eye.

"I don't know. Twenty-five?" I guessed.

She giggled. "Hell no!" she cussed loudly as I darted my eyes to Washburn and Robinson. No reaction.

"I'm thirty-two years old going on a hundred and thirty-five." This made me giggle. So did she.

"A hundred and thirty-five? You're crazy, Bourdon." I smiled. "And this is your first year of teaching?"

"It's my second. I was at Tucker High School in Richmond last year. Yeah, you'd think I should be teaching ancient history 101 considering my age. No, I left Tucker because I was stirring up trouble with the powers that be—you know, parents, principals, veteran teacher-know-it-alls. I thought Louisa would be far enough away to let me do what I want to do."

I wanted to ask her what she meant, but the shrill of the bell made me jump. Frankie snuffed her cigarette out.

I blurted out, "Why'd you leave the Navy?"

"Come on, libear!" She smacked me on the back of the head. "You can't ask me, and I can't tell you. The traditions can't be broken, just like the silence!" She pointed at me, smug, like it was some athletic ritual. I pointed back at her and smiled.

"Hey, you all right, libearian? I thought you might have jumped out of your skin just now?" she asked. I nodded. My jumpiness was my first insight into her sensitivity. "Guess it's 'bout time to get back. You come here often?" she asked.

"Fort Apache?" I shuffled in my seat and began to get up. Measuring her sarcastic eyes, I said, "Why yes, some of the most interesting characters in town come here. People from all over have heard about the great Apache walls. Careful, though, you never know who you'll run into here."

"Well," she said making it up from her seat, "I've run into you, now, haven't I?" She winked at me. Looking for the reaction from the departing crones, I looked back at her—coast clear. But she was already walking away. "Later on, libear." And with that she cornered a corner and was gone. Dating was not easy I thought and so fast. In my heart though, I thought our first date went really well even if she was clueless it was one. Total time with her—about two seconds. I didn't want it to end. Suddenly, the library grind of two to a table seemed miserable to me.

Old Frankie Bourdon. A hundred and thirty-five. Goofy.

That cracked me up, and I barely knew her. I was such a gym teacher cynic. I really was. Holden was with me again. This time I wished for a red hunting cap, mainly because I wanted to hide my face and my hair. Suddenly, I was very aware of how I looked. My five-four frame was stung with bees for boobs, my belly was an ad for a flop contest with three large rolls. My legs like pencils, Faber for sure. I was going to have to get with old Luce to figure out a way to make myself look better.

"You know she has a girlfriend, don't you?" Lucy sat down on her couch opposite of me and flicked on the TV.

"What?" My stomach seized up. "I thought Elsie said she didn't. You guys didn't tell me that!" I looked at her.

"She was wrong," she said. Digging deep into her bowl of ice cream, she surfed the channels and twiddled at her toes between which balls of cotton were stuffed. The big night out at Freddy's was beginning to take shape with the beauty rituals. Seventies night was an every-other-weekend event everyone attended, and Lucy started in the morning and spent all day mastering the best she could look. Lucy's hair was wrapped in a towel, and she had no makeup on. Her large, bulbous nose protruded out with a nice gin blossom on the end of it—too much vodka. Luce was short like me but plumper and darker. Her pear-like shape was always shadowed by her ability to keep herself pretty and dressed to the nines. She worked at the skin, the hair, the nails, the makeup. Oy. The Jewish dyke of a drag queen was the best image I could summon. The party girl in her was always looking for girls and fun and any kind of controversy. Women swarmed to her because of her incisive humor.

"Yeah, I think Brock told me that she's been seeing the same girl for going on two years now, but from what he said, he doesn't think they are very happy. You know lesbians and two years, it's like endorphin-giddy city for the first year, U-haul or not, then the demons arrive and the second year is how or what the other person is or isn't—control, control, control. Since there ain't no children or contract, who cares! We're all so incestuous anyway. It's on to the next suspecting or unsuspecting friend of the friend of someone's girlfriend and the cycle starts all over again. This is why I believe in serial monogamy. It's the only thing that works and everyone is happy. Psychiatrists stay in business, and there's always some ring of interesting dyke drama. It's my total will for living." Luce giggled and turned to CNN.

I looked blankly at the TV and then got a beer from the kitchen. I lit a cigarette by Lucy's bay window where an autographed picture of Ellen (Lucy's idol) stared at me. Suddenly, I didn't think anything was funny.

Lucy looked up from her nail tutelage. "Hey, Veer, you seen these tapes they released from that high school shooting? Aren't you even scared to show up to work sometimes?"

"Yeah, I have a hard time matching clothes. That's scary enough to make me want to stay at home sometimes." I was crestfallen and logically knew it was asinine to be so. Intent on her hotpink nailpolish, Lucy focused. She was going to light up the night with her bad self. Night for me—Gracie. "Who's Brock?" I fumbled out.

"Frankie's best friend. I know him from the whole nursing thang. He works at St. Mary's. A twitty one but excellent at what he does. I've met him at a couple of functions, he's funny as hell. He does a great imitation of Barbra Streisand." Lucy's knowledge of the homosexual divas and divettes was apparent, always.

"What do you mean, twitty?" I asked.

Blowing on her nails, "He's the drag attraction once a month at Freddy's. Queen Bees for the afternoon Tea Dance. Boys and girls love him. You should come with me. He told me that we should do a Barbra-k.d. lang combo together. I'm gonna call myself Constance Craving. What do you think? Too much?"

I laughed and stared out the window. Two more blows on the nails, and Lucy was done with phase one of her Saturday ritual of getting-ready-to-get-loaded. "Luce?" I asked.

"Yeah," she stood up to show me the finished product.

"Have you ever looked at me?"

"Looked at you? What do you mean?" She slipped on some flip-flops.

"You know, looked at me?" I put my hands akimbo, then pointed to my face.

"Veer, are you asking me if I've ever been attracted to you? Because if you are, I'd have to say that, yes. That one time we were singing John Denver's 'Country Roads' after a twelve-pack of Budweiser and you didn't know some of the words and I couldn't believe it and then you threw your head back and laughed like a banshee on acid. That would be a definite attraction beer goggle moment. Otherwise, no." She smiled and then stared at me. "Are you okay?"

Welling up in my eyes were tears of sorry. Sorry for myself was big on my list this morning, and I couldn't help it. Lucy put her arms around me and asked me what was wrong.

"I know this sounds silly, but I feel so ugly. I feel like no one will ever be attracted to me or think I'm pretty. My hair is flat and cut like a boy's and my stomach has three rolls when I stand up and six when I sit down and my nose juts up in the air and people at the drive-through think I'm a man and I should shop at a Garanimals for adults store because I never know how to match so I just wear this." I pointed at my simple outfit of black-and-white T-shirt, jeans and tennis shoes. Lucy put her hand to her mouth and laughed.

"Vera Curran! You do shop at the Target, you know. And the thing with matching is in your head because you're too lazy to try anything else."

"Yeah, I guess you're right." I hugged her back and wiped away the sorry tears.

"If you are worried about attractive girls liking you, Vera, then you just have to be patient and use those verbal skills of yours. You can catch 'em with that.

"Why don't you come down to Freddy's with me tonight. I'll introduce you to Brock. Usually he's there after his shift. You'd like him. He's into poetry and Stephen King and all. And, the bonus is this—he's buddies with your Bourdon girl."

"She's not my girl," I said flatly.

"Well, you want her to be, don't you?"

I smacked Lucy on the butt, and she danced away to the bathroom singing something by k.d. lang. In my heart of hearts I knew that I didn't have a chance in hell at getting a kiss from the Frankie girl. But, maybe we could be friends, and I could just imagine every now and again. Maybe that would have to be good enough for me. Lucy, I'm certain, felt the same way.

Yelling into the air, "By the way, I hate Stephen King. The clown thing is just too nutty for me."

"Well, are you coming out tonight or not?" Lucy was holding a bottle of mascara and eyeliner. "You know, when a girl feels down about her looks, there's always makeup. I can do you up and style that 'do of yours."

"I don't think it will help."

"Suit yourself. Lots of girls out tonight. Bourdon might be there, you know. Hmmm?"

Getting up from the seat I had taken in her kitchen, I moved toward the door. "I wish I had known the truth about her girlfriend." A car pulled up. By the racket, I could tell it was

Alma's Plymouth Horizon. I opened the door and told her not to come in.

"Lucy's committed suicide, Alma. Don't bother coming in." I yelled this to her as she dithered up the sidewalk talking about something she'd read in the paper. Passing through the front door, I continued my tirade. "I'm just cleaning up the mess here, Alma. Come back tomorrow, and we'll divvy up the Mary Kay."

Looking disgusted, Alma said, "Real funny, Vera. Are you going out with us?" Out-of-date Obsession perfume lingered, and Alma's hair was higher than usual. She flopped on the sofa.

"I don't know . . . call me later, guys." And with that, I was out the door.

Two cigarettes later, I stopped at a local grocery and bought a six pack. Drinking the first one on the drive home, I listened to k.d. lang. Lucy always made an impression on me. "Country Roads." John Denver. Good God.

I dreamt with a copy of *The Outsiders* face down on my chest while Gracie snored by my side.

Late afternoon on a wintry day, a party of lipstick lesbians and flannel dykes galvanized itself around a fireplace at Alma Lourdes house. When people moved around, the slow motion is surreal and interfaced with black and white molecules of something binary, illogical. Panning the room from above it all, I was both in and out of the party's reality—the omniscient viewer having my brain and body infused with the fuzziness and excitement of the possibility of the night and the dream and the people.

Walking toward me was Frankie. With beer in tow, she bounced from woman to woman while I watched her without embarrassment. Without notice, my stomach felt again like Captain Kirk's did a long time ago when I was seven years old.

Eyes from the Mediterranean, large white teeth, a slight gap, dimples aligned to her mouth like an e.e. cummings parentheses. This piracy of mine—a stolen look—strengthened my resolve to move close to her. The hands around her cup became the hands around my breast. The smile on her face was the thrill of her lips against my cheek. The legs like cement in her jeans lay on top of my hips and pressed firmly into me. Stomach to stomach, breast to breast, face to face, the wondrous length of woman was naked on me and warm and dark and secret. Then, Alma stopped me dead.

"Listen, Veer, I'd stay away from her if I were you," she pushed her glasses up. Lucy walked into the room with her baton and a sash that said "Constance Craving."

"You think?" I ask.

"I don't think. I know. Take a look around, she's way out of your league," Alma said as she watched Lucy saunter by.

Alcohol and dimming lights thickened the consciousness of the party. (Gracie nudged me. Not now, I thought). Interfaced between the party and Gracie's gentle whinings, I awakened to the gentle spin of a spider crawling across my arm. Orbiting into the air, I slapped at it hard while my cartoon heart pounded through the walls of my rib cage.

Chapter 5

After Lucy and Alma told me that Frankie had a girlfriend, I spent much of October and November trying to stop fantasizing about her and our first date and how well everything had gone. The days came and went at Louisa High, and I stayed semi-happy as I worked on doing what I was good at doing—reading, researching, smoking and drinking beer with Gracie-Mac. If you ask me, it was the luck of my strange life here in this county, at this school, in the library. And, even though I took measures to try to get the young PE teacher out of my mind, the Post-it notes, much to my surprise, continued to litter my mailbox with both covert and overt messages.

On some days, I would get a simple note like *hey, libear, have a great day*. Other days they would be *meet me out back, libear.* It sometimes sounded like a Melissa Etheridge song. Silly notes emblazoned a message prefaced with *What do women do?* The follow up came in verb forms like *women burp* or *women yodel* or *women leap over bleachers.* I would respond back with *women can't match* or *women go around the bend* (me after a bad night of drinking with Lucy and Alma) or *women rinse and repeat.* Stupid stuff like that. She stole smokes from me at Apache. Meeting her there with Washburn and Robinson became a weekly ritual. Long legs would trudge by the library, and I would give her a wave. She back to me with a common signal near the close of the day on her free period to meet for a smoke. In the silence of my old heart, I began to live for the notes and the minutes with her at Apache. We were becoming friends. Good enough. Simple as that. It would have to be acceptable.

Toward the end of the semester, I counseled Holt on the mysteries of the Bible and the parts where homosexuality were spoken ill of. I gave him the range of Sodom and Gomorrah, Leviticus, Paul's Letter to the Romans and a smattering of others. Consideration always, I said to him, must be to analyze both the right and left wings of things. Conservatives will lean more toward the literal "God's Word" approach whereas liberals will bank on the "how the passages are interpreted" approach. People hate, I told him, because people are ignorant and misinformed and the intellectuals who hate are, by and large, in a competition to have their thinking and logic validated by the masses, like a power trip of sorts. Lisping out his thanks, Holt walked away and helped his group earn a strong B on the semester's history project. Frankly, I didn't care about the Bible or the masses or who thought what about what. My shame was firmly rooted in my mother's madness.

Four days before Christmas break, I had an urgent Post-it in my box. A miniature orange cone was taped to the note. Giggling, I swiftly read the usual opening line—*What do women do?* Then it said *Women get fucked by their mothers.* At the end it said *Meet me at Fort Apache after school.* After school—wow! Something was definitely up. My stomach dropped. Eileen Bourdon, the school's prayer leader and member of the school board. Christian coalition flashed in front of me. Hmmm . . .

Hours dragged by, and Carol got on my last nerve trying to get organized for the big Christmas Poetry of Lights festival we put on every year for all of the study halls to come and see. Basically, we lit up the library with fake candles and Carol gets dressed up like Mrs. Claus and reads from Clement C. Moore's poem "Twas the Night before Christmas" or some Kwanzaa tribal boom-boom spoken word thing. Throughout the day, the faculty and classes would show up to our very big deal. Principal Dixon would put on an elf hat and read something Christmas-y or season-y that he picked for the final faculty meeting before break. Usually a huge snorer. All anyone wanted to do was to get the hell out of Louisa High School and go home and plop down for two weeks before coming back to the drudgery and grind of six more months till June.

Finally, I lit up at the Fort. It was 3:45 p.m. Bourdon was late. I smoked two more while reading from a journal article about F. Scott Fitzgerald before she showed up.

"Libearian!!!" She zoomed around the corner in gym-teacher-swishy-pant style. "Got a smoke?" Thievery. Always taking mine.

"Bourdon, where the hell you been? I was getting worried that they had closed up the bleachers and you were underneath." Handing her a cigarette, I noticed her eyes were puffy. She ran her hands over her chest, felt in her pockets for a lighter till I eventually handed her a book of matches from the table.

"They closed me up in the bleachers yesterday. I felt like paper going through a fax. Only two hours to get out." Turning to her side, she smiled. "Skinnier, don't you think?" I nodded then looked away.

"Listen, Bourdon, what's up with the mini-cone and the problem with your mom. Is everything okay?" Exhaling, she sat down at the table opposite me and looked at the sky. She was pensive, almost melancholy. This woman she was to speak of conjured a metaphorical distaste in my mouth.

"Vera." She never called me anything but "libear" or "libearian." Some weird teddy bear association I always thought. A quivering lip made me want to reach out and hold her hand, but I only managed to look at her as lovingly as I could.

"Yeah, Bourdon," I said back. "Are you okay?"

"Vera—" She paused. Now her hands were shaking, and I was getting nervous. "Do you know who my mother is?"

"Yeah, she's the queen of the flagpole. I see her every day out front with Holt Meyers and Maggie Winterfield—the prayer entourage circling the flagpole. Why?"

"Well, she's become my biggest freak-show of a mom. The Muhammed Ali against my personal battle." She looked back up at the sky. I looked to see what she was looking at then she said, "My biggest nemesis."

"That's a big word for a gym teacher, Bourdon." I tried to joke, but she didn't laugh.

"Vera, do you want to hear this or not?" I could tell she wasn't kidding.

"I'm sorry. Go on." I lit another. We were always blowing smoke signals, I thought.

"Well, you know the VEA has a gay chapter here in Richmond."

"Bourdon, shooooosh, you're talking too loud. Someone will hear you."

"I don't give a fart if they can hear me to the tippy top of the

Rocky Mountains!" she barked. I got up and looked around to see if anyone was near—student or teacher.

"Vera. Sit down and listen, you homophobe," she commanded. "If it will make you feel better, I will keep it down." Stung by her accusatory tone, I sat down. She ground her cigarette out in the tin in front of me.

"My mother is the biggest Christian right-winger in the whole state of Virginia it seems like. She thumps her morals and ideals at the First Baptist Church on Monument Avenue. You know, the one they have on TV every Sunday." I nodded. "Is this interesting?" I nodded again. "So, her newest mission is to not only take on school prayer and the pledge of allegiance but, but, but"—she looked to the sky again—"she's taking on family life and sex education." She stopped there.

I was confused. I waited as she looked at me, then I dumbly said, "So?"

"Where did I lose you?" came the retort.

"The sex part," I said. "I understand the school prayer and pledge, but not the sex education piece."

"LIBEARIAN! Who do you think teaches sex education at this school? I'm the one who's been secretly trying to get homosexual family life taught here."

"Now there's a pun unintended—secretly getting homosexual family life here." I bellied out a guffaw.

"That's the reason I left Tucker High School last year. Too much red tape. I figured a smaller school district would be better. You know, no one would notice. Like an idiot, I forgot my mom was on the school board. Now, she's taking over the prayer circle here. I can't shake her wherever I go."

She puffed away and didn't say anything for what seemed like an eternity. Walking around the corner were Washburn and Robinson. Both were enthralled in a conversation about what some kid did to one of the cafeteria workers and how she was going to be suspended for a week. Crossing her eyes and looking right at me, Frankie rolled her eyes. Finally, she asked for my number and said she'd call over holiday break. She walked away as quickly as she arrived.

"You remind me a little of Frankie's mom," I said to my mother.

"Well, isn't that just great. Make me the bad guy." She pushed the chicken in the oven.

"Mother, I'm sorry. She isn't evil, just lost," I said and wondered why I said it at all.

"Good God. How can that be? Isn't she a *saved* woman?" Incredulous, she picked up an onion and began slicing.

From the other side of the counter Kyle pulled up a barstool. "Tell us about her," he said.

I look at the picture on my windowsill and thumbed the small Argentine cross hanging around my neck. The picture is of Lucy, Brock, Alma, Frankie and me in Key West in 1999 at Sunset Cafe at the end of Duvall Street. Our victory trip—well, it was Frankie's.

Slicing away at the onion as if she were on a war mission, Mother chimed in, "Kyle, don't you have some other schoolwork to do or something? Your aunt is getting tired from all this talk."

"I'm all right, Mother. Just a little sad."

Kyle grabbed Grace's leash. "We can pick it up in the morning. I'll take Mac for a walk, and then I'll help with getting dinner on the table." He got up and jetted out the door.

"I'm really okay, Mother. He just wants to write this story down for his psychology class. I'm just helping." I plopped down on the barstool and picked up some peanuts. "Hey, let's eat on the deck."

"Psychology class. Well, you both need your heads examined if you're going to do a report on all that nonsense. None of it makes any sense to me." I ignored her and popped a peanut into my mouth.

After a moment, she finally said, "The deck is fine. That'll be fine. Do you want to set the table?" I nodded and popped another into my mouth. The picture flashed back to me, and for a second I daydreamed about Key West. My eyes created surface tension with my own salty water—not with this woman before me. I walked away from mother, the need to be alone surpassed the need to have obligatory dinner talk.

An hour later, the three of us sat down to Southern cooking done the Momma way. The baked chicken took center stage, and the smell of it mingled in with the soft scent of my sheltering pines. For a moment, I thought my mother might be Demeter and I Persephone, and she had just rescued me from the underworld, and now we were having my redemption dinner. But it was the fall and the mythic tale only played its redemption song in the spring.

Redemption is like labor.

With voracity, Kyle ate while his elbows remained on the table. He secretly gave scraps to Grace who stood panting under the table. Mother caught him and gave him a kick. He smiled and winked at me. What a good young man he was, I thought. Still, that hair.

"Aunt Vera," he managed to say between stuffing his mouth, "can you tell us now about Frankie's mom and how all that stuff happened out at Louisa High School. Is it okay to ask?"

Mother chimed in, "Can we just have a peaceful dinner without bringing up what happened. Do you all want to send me into orbit? I already feel like I've been there. Jesus Christ, Vera! Do we have to revisit all that?"

I ignored the plea. "Where did I leave off, Kyle?" Momma sighed and looked away in disgust. She stabbed at her chicken, fell silent and eventually left me alone.

"It was Christmas break, and she just told you about her mom being on the school board and the sex education part." Kyle gave Grace another scrap. At this, Momma got up and went to eat in the kitchen. Sex and gay topics always made her uncomfortable. Some things never change.

"Well," I said, "it was then that Frankie got interested in the Bible. She needed more information about it because it was her mother's main reference on just about everything. You see, Frankie was an active member of the VEA's gay alliance for teachers and she was an advocate for the inclusivity of the teaching of safe sex and homosexuality in her sex ed classes."

"They never taught me about homosexuality when I was in high school," Kyle interjected. "All they talked about was anatomy and where babies came from, basically."

"Right," I added. "You see Frankie was really upset that the curriculum left homosexuality out completely. When she began to voice her concerns in December, her PE comrades became suspicious of her."

"You mean they thought she was a lesbian?"

"Not only did they think she was a lesbian, but a few of them began to document everything she did. It was strange. Her friends in the department began to turn against her." I paused. "Do you want some pie?" He shoved a last hunk of chicken into his mouth and nodded. Oh, yes, I mouthed to him.

"I'll get it." And, he was off to the kitchen, handing Grace a few bites all the way.

His curiosity about the last few years of my life was refreshing.

Out to the left of my deck I looked at the path that rolled itself through the two big pine trees that Grace was always digging under. Hanging in the air were remnants of Virginia humidity, the kind of humidity that breathed itself in during early spring only to exhale, finally, in September. Tonight, it lingered. It was like breathing in sap sometimes—always glueing itself to the lining of lungs and the follicles of every hair and pore. Two blackbirds jetted by as Gracie eyed a squirrel. I picked up some twigs from a basket on the deck and lit my chimenea with my cigarette. Pensive thoughts and dark eyes were what filled my lungs these days.

"Here we go. Apple pie á la mode. Now who could beat that?" Kyle sat next to me and looked out at Gracie. "How many holes has she dug around that pine, Aunt Vera?"

"Well, if you ask me, I think it's enough to make a golf course or two. Want to do some putting?" I joked. "Now where were we?" Kyle reached for his notes.

I began again, this time paying attention to the details I needed him to write down and for my heart to conjugate.

"Christmas of 1998 came like all the ones had had before. Except, if you ask me, this one was different. I began to spend time with the leggy Bourdon gym teacher and she with me. I was worried about spending time with her because I didn't know much about sports and PE and such. But, I gave her insight into the King's English. Literary Vera trying to impress her. In the middle of one of my oral epistles on Emerson, I believe, she once looked at me like I was the brightest person in the world. I'll never forget it. Anyway, she said that when I talked prose and poetry, it made her feel whole in her universe, whatever that meant, that kings and queens and dukes and duchesses and fairies and myths and fables and parables and the like had survived the history of man. I said woman, too. With a high five, she agreed and smiled her smile at me. Odd, I began teaching her without even knowing it. Such a simple thing, you know, to teach her.

"Several days before Christmas, she called. I think it was then that she began to like me."

"She began to like you then?" Kyle shoved in a bite. "Didn't you say that she had a girlfriend?" Pie fell to the plate on that question. Good one.

"Yeah, but it didn't matter. She was, at that point, on her way out—"

Kyle interrupted. "Frankie's girl?"

"Yes. And, even though it took quite awhile, I believe I was on my way in. It was around then that I met her buddy Brock. Oh my! What a character he was, speaking of queens and duchesses."

"Handsome?" Kyle asked, feeding pie to Gracie from his fork.

"An Adonis," I said. "Now, I'm not good at men's looks, but this guy is up there with the Greeks for sure. Women who love Tom Cruise would drool. And the good part is that he is a nurse who does drag. Imagine that, a Cruise look-alike who does drag."

"Well, didn't Lucy say he was kind of twitty?"

"Don't believe everything Lucy says. He was only slightly twitty, but endearing enough. I call him the Q-man." I giggled.

"What? Q for Queer?" Kyle asked.

"No. Q for quotes. He loves quotes, any quotes. 'Bite my ass' is his favorite incisive barb." I looked to the sky.

"Have you heard from him lately?"

"Brock? Oh, yes. Brock calls me all that time. That queer! But it was my first call from Frankie I remember most."

• • •

"Veraaaaa!"

"Helloooooo," I said, thinking there is a crazy woman on the other end.

"What the hell are you doing? It's me Frankie!"

"I know who it is, you crazy girl."

"It's Saturday! What are you doing?" she yelled.

"Reading some book about women who run with the wolves!"

"Jesus! Are you kidding? What's it about?"

"Why are you yelling?"

"It's Saturday, and I'm coming to get you. I always yell because I think no one is listening. No offense. The night hag Brock is hung over. I have kidnapped his ass. I have three packs of Marlboros, an old Kate Bush tape and lots of leather on! He's jealous because I look better in leather than he does."

From the background I heard, "Bite my ass, PE dyke." Brock Goldberg with a wet cloth on his face. I could almost see it.

With this, I half swooned like I did in September when I tried to get her to read a poem about some stupid tree in Louisiana at the gay advocacy meeting. Reading a book about finding your inner wolf, your inner nature, it's ironic. I wanted to howl, but all I managed was a sheepish clearing of my throat.

"Where are we going, Bourdon?"

"Listen, libear. Don't worry. I'll come and get you. You already told me before you have a lousy sense of direction. I'll be there, say, in thirty minutes."

I giggled. She was right. I could barely get to school and back without getting lost. And, merging on the interstate was something never broached. "But, wait. I have to wash my hair."

"Christ, libear. This isn't some date. Are you on?"

"I'm on. We'll be women who ride in cars," I threw out the allusion before remembering she may not know the meaning.

"We'll be women who ride in cars," she echoed me back not caring about allusions at all.

From the background, "How about education dykes who run with the trucks is more like it."

Then, a sidebar. "Bite my ass Q-man." Frankie yelled some more.

Then a muffled response. "Let me get my leather peeler out. It may take awhile." Chiming in I say, "Are you talking to me? Why are you talking so loud?" I asked again, laughing.

"Because I love your libearian's ass, and I feel like it!" She said this, she actually said this.

With a Tourette response back, I yelled, "I love your ass, too!" I didn't know what else to say. I gave her directions. Click. That was it.

I dialed Lucy to ask about clothing. She had awoken with a similar hangover. Drinking with Brock and Bourdon I found out. I tried for a few details about the night, but she could barely get her cotton mouth unglued to utter a Garanimal match for me. She gave me some basics then told me we'd hook up for coffee later.

I didn't have the Bohemian outfit Lucy had described to me. Settling for an extra large white T-shirt and extra large Levi's and my black Reeboks, I washed my hair. In New York City, I would have screamed fashion redneck idiot. In Virginia, I would fit in at any strip mall as the one no one sees.

Forty minutes later, a Toyota pickup truck ground the ruts out in my driveway. When I jetted out of my front door, I saw that it would be a tight squeeze. Gracie whined because I forgot her biscuit. I ran back to the foyer and grabbed one off the box on the table and gave it to her.

Waving to Brock and Frankie, I looked to the ground to find my feet, my footing. I sucked in my stomach and put my hand through my still wet hair. Clutching the wallet in my front pocket, I opened the door and saw Frankie with a beer in between her legs and a cigarette on her lips and the most hung over handsome man I've ever seen—Brock Goldberg. His head was back on the seat, and he cocked his head toward me and said, "Hello, I'm Brock." Raspy voice from a night of shooters and beer chasers, I assume. A beer lingered between his legs, too. Suddenly, I felt scared. I was getting in a truck with Bonnie and Clyde, although I wasn't sure who was who.

Frankie hopped out and whacked me on the shoulder, "Hey, hair looks nice. Jump in."

"Where are we going?" I asked and scooched into the middle.

Brock looked up. "We're doing a drive-by of Frankie's mom's house—"

Frankie interrupted, "And then we're going to Freddy's for mucho grande beers and cigarette smoking galore and loads of conversation about our very important lives!"

"Are we going in?"

"Where, Freddy's? Come on, libear, how else are we getting Bloody Marys? My mom isn't serving any alcohol."

I dropped it.

Frankie sped down Route 250 and spent the first few minutes fumbling with the tapes. When she found the one she wanted, she yelled my name, something she rarely did, "Vera!"

"Bourdon, I'm sitting right here. Why are you yelling?"

"Making sure you are paying attention!" She turned and looked at me for a split second. The flash melted me in the middle. I held the look, then panicked and looked ahead.

"Bourdon, you're crazy. You know that?" I look at Brock who

rubbed a wet cloth over his face. He paid no attention to our babble.

"I know, libear, that's why you like me."

"You know, I just don't go riding around with anybody," I joked.

"This is the music right here"—she flashed the tape in front of my face—"*Amplified Heart.* The best driving CD ever."

"Amplified what?"

"Here, libear." She swigged her beer. "Listen." She popped it in.

Brock lifted his head. "What's this last name business you two are engaging in? It sounds like you're Army buddies or something." He drank his beer, looked at Frankie then me, and put his head back on the seat. "Jesus, Frankie, could you not drive so fast. Freddy's will still be there, and your mom is a goddamned monument herself. We aren't going to miss anything—"

"Oh, Brock, shut up and drink your beer. I'm buying you lunch anyway, you queer polecat."

"I'm not old. And, don't call me a polecat, you, you bean curdetta," Brock turned the music up.

"What's a bean curdetta?" I asked. Brock opened me a beer and handed it to me. Now I was an accessory.

"I don't know. It just sounded like something grandiosely small and insignificant. So, you and the Frankster work together. What do you do?" He now looked like a pinball going from her to me, me to her in the conversation.

"Librarian," I swigged with him, "I'm a librarian at Louisa High and—" and before I could get out the next word it seemed as if Brock had gone into an apoplectic stroke, right in front of me.

"Ohhhhh, myyyyy, Gooood! You're a librarian?" He was like

a Kate Chopin awakening. He pointed at me then uh-huhed his own point. "That's *oh my god*!" He patted his pecs in an ironically twitty fashion. Frankie laughed at him then sloshed back her beer. I looked for the police who, I was now sure, were following us. I looked for a James Bond eject button. These two were for real. He continued. "So, you read a lot of books and stuff?"

"Yes, I do, but—"

Frankie interjected, "Brock, settle down. You'll bust a seam or something." Frankie looked at me again and rolled her eyes.

"Listen here, PE dyke, the only one busting a seam in this truck is you with your painted-on leather." He turned to me. "Do you like quotes?" I couldn't answer before he continued. I took another drink and stared at him. "I love quotes," he went on. "I read one everyday. I have a whole stack of good ones at home that I try and keep abreast of." He patted his chest. "Here's one. 'Life is what happens to you while you were making other plans'." He sounded serious. It was strangely farcical. I wanted to laugh in his face but contained myself. "Do you know who said that one?"

"Joan of Arc," I responded tersely.

"No, silly. John Lennon." The roll was just beginning. "How about this one. 'Don't eat more than you can lift.' Know this one?"

"Elizabeth Taylor."

"Good one, libear," Frankie steadied her eyes on the road.

Brock swooned in the spotlight, "No. It was Miss Piggy." He was elated, and we all laughed and at once drank from our beers.

"Libear, do you know how to dance?" Frankie said suddenly.

"Like with your arms and feet?" I asked.

"What?"

"Like with your arms and feet?" I asked again.

"Like with arms in *wheat*?" she repeated.

"No, like with your ARMS and FEET!" I tried to yell.

"Good God, can you speak up. You must be the most soft-spoken person I know."

"Part of my charm, I guess," I looked out the window.

Brock came alive again, "Okay, here's one. It's Vera, right?" I nodded. " 'Parting is such sweet sorrow'."

I tried to yell. "Shakespeare. *Romeo and Juliet.* Juliet to Romeo in Act III." Then I looked wildly out the window.

"I knew you would get that one," Brock leaned forward and looked at Frankie. "I knew she would get that one." He was satisfied. Completely.

"How did you know all that, libear?" Frankie asked.

"I didn't tell you that I taught English for fifteen years before taking on the coveted role as librarian extraordinaire? You name it, I think I taught it."

Brock opened another beer. "How many fags did you teach? They say there are at least one in ten, so, you must have had a few."

"Where we work, the parents beat it out of the kids before first grade," I said.

Frankie cruised closer to the city limits and pressed me again. "Do you know how to dance?"

"No, Bourdon. I don't. That's the second time you've asked. How come?"

"Vera Curran, don't tell me you don't know how to dance," she emphatically stated, leaning over to look at Brock.

"Bourdon, I don't. I really don't." I'm half ashamed. "No one ever taught me. I failed cotillion and basketball. No coordination at all."

"Brock?" Frankie was still leaning forward.

"Yeah, dahlin'," he leaned forward too.

"Looks like we're going to have to teach this lady how to dance," she said with certainty. She is confident, but I have no rhythm. They would see.

"Listen. Brock and I will teach you how to dance if you teach me about the Bible."

Brock opened another beer for me. "Oh, God, here we go again." He looked at me and rolled his eyes.

Incredulous, I took the beer. "What? The Bible?"

"Yeah, the Bible. The book that's been screwing up homos for a few thousand years. Remember? Our talk? Fort Apache? It's about mom and this education thing. I have been fighting an uphill battle ever since I came out to her, and now it's gotten worse."

Brock interjected, "She's the kind that believes Matt Shepard got what he deserves."

"When did you tell her you were gay?" I asked.

Cradling her ear with her hand, she screams, "What!!!"

"WHEN DID YOU TELL HER YOU WERE GAY?"

Frankie smiled. "Verbally or graphically?" She thought she was a comic. We turned another corner and before I knew it, we were in a historic part of Richmond where cobblestones bobbled the wheels of the truck. Like attentive soldiers guarding the streets, row houses lit a path of Christmas lights and a luminescence exuded from the dirty genealogical tragedies harbored like ghosts in the homes, in the alleys and in the air. Shrines of Civil War markers made the covert prejudice still complete.

"Okay, both verbally and graphically," I stated.

Frankie stiffened then took her bottle of courage up and swigged it into her mouth. "Well, I outed myself early on. I guess around three or four. It was Christmas and my mom had spent a lot of cash on some dolly. When I opened it up and looked at it, I promptly handed it over to my sister. I was truly bucking for a G.I. Joe and bow and arrow. This was the first graphic, the first visual that something might have been up."

Suddenly, I asked where her mother lived.

"Right in Church Hill. Ironic, eh. I mean isn't that a bit of irony?"

"More like parallelism." I noted a wince of pain deep within her. I sensed something more was there but let the conversation go on. Brock was listening, but he was also glancing through the window at some men on the street. My belief was that their friendship was deep, a secure familial love. "Then what," I said.

"Then . . . I was a kid. Twenty-two. In love." She paused. "I walked out on my momma's screen porch on Easter Sunday. I was crocked from a party on Monument Avenue. You know, every year there's a big parade, and I thought it might be a good time to let the folks know. A gorgeous day, everyone was out and about. There were bands and people with bonnets and games and funnel cakes. My girlfriend and I had walked down the great Monument Avenue. I was utterly and completely in love, and I thought I might just tell the old bat, you know?"

"Yeah," I added, "I know."

"Well, I came out on the porch. I tell you, she really killed my buzz. So, I say, 'Hey old bat, I got something to tell you.' She came out onto the porch in her Sunday best and said the first thing she always says when I call her the old bat: 'Frankie? Frankie, how much beer have you had to drink. Lord, I can see you're drunk. You drink too much little girl.'

"Why she said 'little girl,' I don't know 'cause I'm not small. Anyway, she stared at me with pursed lips, and I just came right out and said, 'Four beers, Momma. One for you and the others are for the Father, the Son and the Holy Ghost. I plan on drinking one for ol' Mary, though. She never gets enough credit.' "

Brock and I were riveted. Then I added, "Well, what then?"

"I said, 'Momma, I want you to know I am gay. It's about time you know this. What do you think Jesus would say?' "

Brock came alive again, "Did she faint?"

"No, she didn't. She did the weirdest thing. She grabbed a Bible off of the table and spanked me all the way up the stairs. I laughed and cried and screamed the whole way. She said, 'Frankie, child, you are a disdainful, sick child. Where are your manners and morals? Where are your manners and morals?' When we got to my bedroom where the dolly from fifteen Christmases past sat on my dresser, she grabbed it and flung it at my head. When I opened my eyes, she had a finger pointing at me. With her nostrils flaring, she simply said that I wasn't her daughter that I never was and that I had twenty-four hours to move my diseased bones out of there.

"The wild thing is I just wanted to hug her and hold onto her and tell her it was all right. She for most of my life had been a truly good mom, you know. I loved her. I still love her. God just got in the way instead of helping. He's a very confusing character."

"If you ask me," I said, "he confuses most everyone." With that, Frankie turned into an empty parking lot and threw her truck into park and jumped out. Frozen to our beers, Brock and I watched her walk to a line of leafless trees. For a minute we just sat there, then I finally hopped out. Frankie reminded me about my beer by pointing, and I handed it into Brock who was looking for a new CD. *Amplified Heart* was still echoing from the cracked windows.

With cigarette in hand, Frankie called me by my first name. I now am realizing that when she's serious, it's the real name. When she's not serious, it's libear. Slightly lost, I walked toward her.

"Bourdon, where are we?" I asked, but she ignored me.

"Libearian!" she yelled and threw down her cigarette.

"Yeah." I moved near her and in doing so noticed that we are just below the city lines to Church Hill, the most historic spot in Richmond's history where Patrick Henry gave the big liberty speech. That was irony, I mused. The cold connected to my bones and I shivered. Nerves, too, I reckoned. The smoke and breath from Frankie's mouth was all at once sexual and my stomach, without notice, dropped. My hands found their way to my pockets, and I left them there out of nervousness and cold. A few seconds later, they began to shake violently, making my elbows quiver.

"I need you to help me understand this Bible thing and why it's the front for everyone who hates us. Can you do that? At some point, I'm going to have to go before the school board with my proposal, and if I have a baseline understanding, then I'll feel more comfortable." She put her hands on her hips. "You helped Holt Meyers. Jesus, can you help me?"

"I can't be an accessory to the crime, Bourdon. I don't understand why you and the rest of the Rainbow Coalition just don't wake up and smell the cappuccino. We live in Virginia. HELLO! Plus, I am a Republican who happens to like and believe in a lot of what our political pundits and advocates say. I don't want to fight with you and your mom and the local school board. Hell, I'm so far inside my own closet, I almost considered quitting when Holt Meyers asked me to help him in the first place. You won't win, Frankie. If you ask me, it just isn't possible." I let my honesty fly.

Incredulous at my pronouncement, she just laughed and said, "I'm not asking you if I will win or not. I'm not even asking you to help me with anything but the Bible nuances that screw us up. That's all, libear. You ol' asshole."

I duly noted how tired she looked and then how cold I was getting. In the middle of my impossible life, this young, vivacious gym teacher was asking me for a favor. It was simple coaching I thought.

Finally, I nodded then said, "Yes, I will show you a few things about the Bible, but I'm not a connoisseur, Bourdon."

"VERA!"

I almost fell back. "What, what?!" I looked around for myself.

"I love your ass!"

From the truck, Brock yelled, "Well, bite my ass and get back in the truck. It's freezing, people. You last-name Army men might be used to it, but I'm not!"

Back in the truck, it felt warm all over to have somebody love my ass. It was flat and kind of cottage-cheesy, but nevertheless, I was glad to have someone like it. I patted ol' Frankie on the back and told her that I liked her ass too, but I was not half as loud as she was when I said it. She must have thought I was some Bible scholar, but I was not. When you are a librarian, people think you know everything, but if you asked me, I really didn't know much at all. The only knowledge worth having right now was that this Frankie girl liked me and that was all right with me.

With the newly found revelation that I would teach her about the Bible, the three of us rode to the top of the hill past St. John's Church toward Eileen Bourdon's house. Passing the graveyard in front of the church, I got a surreal feeling that lingered in me long after our day would be over. Frankie opened another beer, and we all made a toast to a quote from Brock—"To life, liberty and the pursuit of happiness, for all dykes, drag queens and librarians." A goddamned comic, that Q-man.

"That's the famous Patrick Henry Church. He was the best spokesperson Virginia ever had," I noted.

"Remind me of the history," Frankie said. "We'll be by my mom's in a minute."

"Well, Henry was quite the man, you know. Especially at the Virginia Convention because a bunch of delegates got together and were talking all wishy-washy about the arms build-up in America and trying to figure out the best way to get the British the heck out of America. So, the namby-pambys are saying this and that, and we're gonna do it this way when ol' Henry gets up and stirs 'em up about how they shouldn't be betrayed by a kiss and that they had eyes to see but weren't seeing much and ears to hear but weren't hearing much and that they'd better wake up before they got a good ass-whipping. It was all extemporaneous. Lore has it that he just got up and went for it and after it was all said and done he said, 'Give me liberty or give me death.' I guess we pretty much rocked and rolled after that one."

Atop Church Hill, we cornered a corner by Chimbarozo Park where the Civil War battle had ensued more than one hundred and twenty years earlier.

"Well, we certainly aren't rocking and rolling in the gay community," Frankie chimed in after a pregnant pause. "I mean we had Stonewall, and I think that's about all mainstream America might remember except for the march on Washington a few years back. Since Stonewall, we've hit a brick wall." The impassioned Frankie made me giggle. I asked her what Stonewall was, and she slapped me on the back of the head. "Vera, don't laugh at me. I'm being serious." She put a cigarette to her lips and lit up. She did one of those French jobs up her nose and I thought she was looking rather Boho so I told her.

"Vera, are you listening? Or do your ears just hear?" Then she blew smoke in my face.

Brock shifted in his seat, caught my eyes and rolled them, evidence that he'd heard this before.

"Frankie, we've come a long way, but remember I voted for Reagan, George Bush and Bob Dole. I'm not some gay activist who's trying to change how America thinks. I'm queer and just happy shelving books in the nine hundreds, smoking my cigs—by the way, give me one—and having a couple of beers every now and then. This is my American dream. Hey, and quit blowing smoke in my face, Bourdon! What do you want, another Rosa Parks at-the-back-of-the-bus movement?"

"It was the front of the bus," Brock corrected.

"There it is." Frankie pointed. The old bat's house. The corner of Three Chopt Avenue and 22nd Street. Frankie parked in front and told Brock and me to stay put.

Corinthian columns supported the front porch of the southern Victorian row house while Christmas lights adorned the spindles around the decking and small concrete cherubs decorated each side of the sidewalk. Eileen Bourdon's house.

"What is she doing?" I asked Brock.

"She's just checking in. Usually, she brings me along for the ride."

"Checking in?" I questioned again.

"Yeah, she just likes to say hi sometimes. I don't know, Vera. It's a love-hate thing between them."

"Does her mom know about the school board thing Frankie wants to fight?"

"Not yet."

"Oh, God," I said.

"Tell me about it."

Frankie came out of the front door and waved us in. Brock

and I simultaneously shook our heads. No way. Then she waved harder and Brock caved. We both put our beers down.

Once inside the house, I felt panic fill my stomach. It made me quiet and still. I listened nervously to the tickings of the house. Eileen Bourdon came in from the kitchen where I supposed she was making poison cookies for the kids at the NAACP's Christmas pageant down the street.

"Hello, Brock. How are you?" she asked as she motioned all of us into the living room.

"You must be Vera. Frankie was just telling me about you. It's so nice to meet you. She tells me that we all have something in common." She stared at me. I sucked in my stomach and knew instinctively that the homo thing was out of the in-common question. The pause stretched for more than enough seconds till Frankie told us both to sit down.

"Louisa High School," I blurted it out, finally. "We all work there."

Eileen eyed me, and I noticed how dark the circles were under her eyes. Her red hair was cut severely around her ears, fashioned in an old Shirley MacLaine-ish way. Slightly thick in the middle, I thought she was attractive. Then, I nuttily imagined she ate only at dinnertime where she lined up her carrots next to her peas and didn't let her meat touch anything.

When she spoke it was right into you as if she had two separate lenses, one for her and her own speech and one to note any and all intimations of her subject's body language and facial expressions. She was a quick study. I crossed my legs to try to be more feminine. Brock noticed and spread his to mock me. "Right, well, you two work at Louisa. I'm just a liaison in charge of community relations for the PTA and the school board. I grew up there before moving to Richmond. I helped Frankie get her job there after she left her job in Richmond last year. Why you left Tucker still puzzles me, Frankie." She paused while glancing furtively her way. "I just love that school. Don't you?" I nodded in agreement. Frankie picked up a magazine from the coffee table and began absentmindedly thumbing through it. "I mean the children are just so lovely and hard working and dedicated."

"Mom, they are high-schoolers. They smoke pot, plagiarize and have sex."

Eileen kept her eyes on Brock and me. "Frankie, you're always so to-the-point. Why don't you get these two some coffee?" To my surprise, Frankie got up and went to the kitchen and abandoned us with her mom who was really quite benign. A striped calico cat entered the room and jumped on Eileen's lap. It purred, and she stroked it gently. It was then that Eileen and I began talking about high school and the politics of teaching the children. Trying not to rock any boat, I maintained a balance of uh-huhs and hmms to garner a bit of appreciation through that second lens of hers. If you asked me, it wasn't too terribly hard. A few minutes later, Frankie entered with a tray of coffee for all of us. She first served her mother, then Brock, then me. When she handed me the coffee, she looked right at me and winked. I smiled and looked at Brock who raised his left eyebrow. He was the consummate observer, I thought.

Frankie sat down with her coffee. Between the caffeine and alcohol, I wasn't sure what was to come out of her mouth next. "So, Mom," she began, "what's up with you and the holidays? Are you working hard at church?"

Eileen centered herself more stiffly on the couch and looked at her daughter. The energy between them was palpable. As I looked at them, I noticed family pictures scattered about the end tables and mantel over the fire place. Old photos, it seemed. A picture of Frankie in the Navy was in a corner by itself near the bay window where a crucifix lay gingerly next to it. Hope, I thought. What the hell did I know.

Eileen sipped her coffee. "Why yes, I'm working with Mr. Winterfield on some homeless dinners and will be taking my prayer group to assist with dishing out the food."

"The prayer group from Louisa?" Frankie asked.

"Yes. They are devoted young kids, I tell you," she looked from Brock to me and then Frankie.

"Vera, do you know these kids?" Frankie looked at me.

I wiped the dribble of coffee from my lips. "Uh, yes. I think it's Holt and Maggie and some of the others from the play. She's right. Nice kids. I just got through getting Holt through one of his history projects. That guy's a hard worker." Oh, God.

"Oh," Eileen interjected. "I'm great at history. What were you helping him on?"

My elbows quivered. I set the coffee cup down and lied right through my teeth. "Oh, it was nothing. Just some work on the Romantics and the history of the Transcendental movement."

"You mean here in America?" Eileen asked.

Brock interjected from his silence, "All good movements happen here in America. Right, Vera? I mean just look at fashion movements in the last one hundred years. From hoop skirts to hoops through your nose." We all laughed. Eileen faked it.

"Frankie, will you be home for Christmas dinner?" she asked.

"Uh, yes. I will."

"Brock and Vera. If you don't have plans then you are welcome to have dinner as well. Frankie and I and her sister usually have a quiet one right here by the bay window. It's beautiful in Church Hill at Christmas. Please do come." I nodded and Brock said that he might.

We finished our coffee and said the usual good-byes. I kept sucking in my stomach and followed everyone from behind.

Once in the truck and off to Freddy's, Frankie laughed. "Libear, romantics and transvestites?"

"Transcendentalists," I interrupted.

"I like transvestites best," Brock lifted his beer up in a toast. "Good God, did you see your mom's outfit?"

"Yeah, why?" Frankie asked. "It's the kind of stuff she always wears."

"Well, honey. She gives new meaning to the phrase 'some stretch pants have no other choice'."

That cracked me up.

"Oh you think that's funny, do you?" She slapped me on the back of the head again.

"Frankie, stop hitting me on the head."

"Oh, you love it." She was right, I did.

It seemed like we cascaded our way through the Hill while breaking every motor vehicle law imaginable. Brock didn't wear a seat belt, we all had open containers, and Frankie ran every stop sign while singing to k.d. lang. Her favorite she told me.

We rode by the eclectic houses that obviously had no covenants attached to them. One block had giant homes donned with white lights and bright red ribbons and candles adorning windows. On the next block, a row house jutted out with signs pitched around the yard quoting the gospel, revelation and the apocalypse. In the side yard was an old rusty grocery cart and a sign that said, "God keeps his promises." Next to that, a toilet with an American flag poking sideways from the base. The contrast was real and creepy.

Here it all was, Frankie's roots. She got to the bottom of the Hill and sped away.

Chapter 6

After we drove around Richmond reminiscing about historical sites I knew and finally arrived at Freddy's, Brock had reeled off a hundred of his famous quotes and had poked more fun at Eileen's outfit. Frankie was cussing like a sailor, and I was half drunk and having more fun than I had had in over ten years. These two had come to get an old librarian from the confines of her country home. I was so happy, as trite as it sounded.

When I walked into Freddy's, I was elated to see Alma and Lucy in a corner booth. They caught my eye, saw who I was with and both—always in simpatico—dropped their respective mouths in dismay.

The sun lowered in the sky, and it cast a shimmering line right through the middle of the bar. I felt certain that I was fraternizing with the gay mafia. I was embarrassed but at the same time comfortable around them—family, I supposed.

Elsie came and gave us a round of margaritas and welcomed us to the Saturday Tea Dance. A new venue because Freddy's was closed most Sundays except on special occasions and holidays where there was money to be made. We settled into our round booth discussion as if we were in Queen Lancelot's court and discussed everything from politics to movies to Lucy's favorite—sex.

Lucy looked really pretty, and Alma's hair was up in a bun—the eternal school teacher in her couldn't help it. Lucy finally asked Frankie what had been on my mind for hours.

"So, Frank, how's it going with you anyway?"

"Lucy, I'm fantabulous," she laughed and looked across the table at Brock and me.

"Well," she giggled, "are we still married?"

Brock licked his salt. "She doesn't believe in marriage, Lucy. She believes in dual destiny."

"Dual destiny?" Alma looked at Lucy for help. "What does that mean?"

Frankie took a long draw from her straw, garnering a cup of courage, I supposed. "Marriage is so flat and Republican"—she looked at me—"and old and contractual, and it smells like old hetero people and—"

Brock interrupted. "God, say *and* one more time and, and, and I'll start hitting you on the back of the head." I laughed and hit Brock on the back of the head just as Frankie had hit me.

Lucy ordered another round. I looked for the police. Elsie asked if we wanted menus with our blood alcohol. We all nodded.

"Frankie," Lucy went on, "you know what I mean. Are you still with your girl?"

"Oh, hell no. I dropped her two months ago when she spent a whole day arguing with me about how I should do the dishes, fold the laundry and hang my toothbrush. Why are people so interested in stuff that *soooo* does not matter. If I throw my clothes over the door and keep my laundry in the dryer and lay my toothbrush on the windowsill, will it all really matter when I die? Who's gonna know. I'm taking only my memories of what I did when I die and how I did them. That's it. And, if I want to remember how fun it was to be a slob, then that is my bidness."

Alma piped in, "I will remember how organized I was." We all just stared at her. "What?" She looked at me and Lucy hit her on the back of the head.

We revisited the sex talk and Lucy discussed the many positions in which she had had her libido stroked. When the talk came to me, I said, mostly with myself, thank you. Frankie cracked up, and I was glad to make her laugh.

After a few more rounds, Frankie launched into the diatribe of her life with Brock as her unfailing assistant. I was certain that after a while a couple of guys named Guido might show up and take us all away.

She began her story with why she wanted to do what she wanted to do with the teaching of homosexuality in the classroom. At first, I wasn't clear on why, but after she traced some life events, it was apparent.

She had been literally and metaphorically struck down by her Bible-wielding mother. In one hand she held it, but on the other, Eileen ran contrary by exclaiming to her daughter that she did indeed love her. When Frankie was young, Eileen Bourdon had scrubbed her daughter's hair over a sink and had inserted pink barrettes and bobby pins and pinched and poked and made her wear dresses and spit-shiny patent leather shoes and go to Holy Communion and listen to the man who replicated Jesus and his garbled tongue of which she didn't understand anything and then put the white wafer in her mouth like she was really eating somebody and now she's accepted Jesus Christ into her life and I hope the poor little tomboy grows out of this stage. My little girl is a tomboy and now look at what she's gone ahead and done to me with playing with her neighbor's Army men and wanting to play the trumpet and listen to Elton John. What kind of appreciation was that?

It was Frankie's lifestyle and how her daughter chose to live it that infused her soul with a rage only known to mothers who had been admonished by their own parents about how and what and who you should be. It was the tooth and nail resiliency, a passion for things that creeped from a standard by which people had gauged and measured themselves for thousands of years. My own relationship to Catholicism, from which I had spent many years trying to shed my skin, was a close parallel—the guilt, the guilt, the incestuous shame, the filth of homosexuality and a woman to boot. It all flung itself on me, and I let it. When Eileen Bourdon started the letter writing campaign she'd seen on TV by a man who had flubbed out his boondoggle and tried to infiltrate Frankie's life and lies with phone calls from people from Chesapeake, Virginia—well, it was then that Frankie got mad. Having just had coffee with her, one would have never known the capabilities of mothers who try to change their daughters with their own agendas because they can't have tea with the women of Three Chopt Avenue without being asked when her youngest daughter was getting married and just why she joined the military. Control. It was all about control and power and perception. Everyone wanted the right perception. I thought of Aldous Huxley and wondered if tripping on acid and unlocking everyone's door of perception might be the right way to thwart change. But, what the hell did I know.

After she had spoken about this, Frankie's own buzz was just getting up to blur. She then said, as if it was the greatest idea in the world, "I really think we ought to start a movement." I laughed. She reached across the table and played like she was going to smack me, but then just played like she was shooting me dead.

"Libear, you don't have to participate. I know you have better things to do like walking your dog and discussing media fairs with Carol and reading books. Real fucking hard, libear. How do you do it?"

Brock saved me. "Tell her to bite your ass, Vera."

"Bite my ass, Bourdon."

Lucy interjected, "I'm always looking for a good movement. Especially if there are plenty of women involved. Alma, what do you think?"

Alma pushed her glasses up with that middle finger. "Well, I don't know. Do we have to get dressed up?"

"I hope so," Brock picked at his head and smirked.

She continued, "I don't know. I'm funny about my profession and getting too involved in the homosexual thing. I just figure someone else will take care of it."

"I think you're looking at it for Virginia, Alma," Frankie spoke up. "I don't know of any VEA gay alliance around here that wants to march with a bunch of teachers supporting the inclusivity of teaching it in the classroom."

"Don't they just learn the homo stuff on the bus?" I asked.

"They learn it like we all did. In the cafeteria, the bathrooms and in the hallways," Frankie said.

Lucy clinked her margarita to Frankie's. "I first made out

with Jewell Lincks behind the baseball dugout. Lots of learning there, my girl. Dugouts are good."

"I learned mine in the locker room," Brock interjected. "Two football players came at me one day, called me a fag and then gave me a swirlie."

"What's a swirlie?" Alma asked.

"They stuck my head in a toilet and flushed till I thought I would drown. Two years after graduation, one of them tried to apologize and pick me up right here in this bar."

"No way," I said.

"Way." Frankie looked at me hard.

"How did you learn, Vera?" Lucy asked.

"Rita Mae Brown came through to me loud and clear in her *Rubyfruit Jungle* tale."

"I never read that," Alma stated.

"Do you read?" Lucy fired back.

"Sometimes. I read textbooks for class and journal articles. Stuff like that."

"Okay, guys. Back to me." Frankie asked for everyone's attention. Elsie showed up with burgers and fries. Alma had her double fries, Lucy her salad. "There's a huge march on Washington in early May of next year. If we start eighteen months ahead of time, then we can effect our own triumphs and tragedies and videotape the whole thing. Maybe they would even give us some mic time on the mall. Come on! We should all start our own local media movement here to get people thinking and then videotape our own."

"Think globally, act locally," Brock bit into his burger and smiled.

"Bite my ass, now, Brock. I'm being serious." Frankie reached for a napkin. "Alma, do you have a pen?" Alma reached into her pocketbook and promptly delivered her one. Always the Girl Scout.

"See, here's the parade route. If we start here, then we can get in line here for open mic."

"How do you know all this when it's a year and a half away?" Lucy asked.

"Dual destiny. It's about meeting the right people and making it all happen. Plus, it helps to have an ex-girlfriend who works for the Human Rights Campaign. She keeps me abreast of the Washington GLBT affairs."

Alma looked at Lucy.

"She means gay, lesbian, bisexual and translucent—like you," Lucy smiled.

Alma smiled back. "No, silly. What is the Human Rights Campaign?"

Frankie slammed her head back on the booth's wall. "Don't tell me you guys don't know that one." I played dumb, too, because I didn't know what it was either. "It's the national coalition that works to give people like you and me equal rights and a voice in government."

Brock spoke up. "They also have the greatest parties each year in D.C., and they host one in March—spring break, the Rainbow Games in Key West. It's hot, hot, hot. HRC has those stickers that look like a blue and yellow equal sign. Frank's got one on her truck, Vera." I nodded.

Lucy mocked Brock and said, "Women, women, women. Alma did you hear?" She looked at me and shrugged her shoulders. Elsie came with another round and said that the Rainbow Games' key event was flag football and that she goes every year.

"Back to me." Frankie directed us back to her. She had the passion of a politician, I thought. "We could all play a role. Luce, you're good at organizing events," she said as she wrote and doodled on her napkin. "Brock, you're good at video and entertaining. Alma you could play backup"—Alma looked at her questioningly—"you know, like a behind-the-scenes gal. You could manage all the items we may need and keep track of them." Alma understood and was relieved. "Vera, you could—"

"I'm not going to go to some march on Washington, Bourdon. I can barely get to the Easter parade here every year. And, that's enough people for me." Everyone ignored me.

Frankie went on, "Vera can write letters and do any research we need." I shook my head. She held up her doodled napkin that displayed what looked like a symbol. A capital W was interfaced with a capital M. We stared at it and then at Frankie.

She simply looked at me and said, "What do women do?" She paused. "Women *move*," she said. I smiled at her.

She was smarter than I thought.

The sun set on the bar while I watched Frankie's strong, veiny hands scribble out more stuff on napkins. She went on to talk about the politics of it all and mentioned again how Stonewall had happened when she was three and how she wanted to be a part of a march when she's an adult, not a kid. This is not Women's Stock 1998, I said to her. She called me a pussy for not wanting to participate. I said that that wasn't so nice to say to me and what would her students say. She said they'd probably agree.

Brock intimated that it will be like a *Butch Cassidy and the Sundance Kid* revival and that he wanted to play the part of Robert Redford's girlfriend. We are criminals, I thought again as he said this. With a rainbow flag in tow, we were to march on Washington and then discuss at an open mic how we need to teach homosexuality in every public high school in America. And, how if we can do it in Louisa County, we can do it anywhere. Right. Louisa County would fire me and Frankie before we could spell G-A-Y the first D-A-Y it came to the school board.

"I'll only help if I can wear a bag over my head and a bulletproof vest," I said and laughed.

"Vera," Alma said, "what are you so afraid of?"

I paused and looked at all of them who are high-fiving and asking me again what I'm afraid of. I am still befuddled by this athletic ritual.

Then I said, "Well, if you ask me—"

"We just did," Frankie winked at me.

"Well, if you ask me, I'm slightly afraid of the truth."

It was like the music had stopped.

"Do you really think, Frankie Bourdon," I continued, "that Louisa County is going to listen to you and your talk about how we should include the teaching of homosexuality in sex ed classes? Do you really think that? I can see it now. The blue-haired ladies from Main Street with their bonnets on, putting white-gloved hands over the big o's on their mouths and covering the eyes and ears of their children at the ruckus you're going to cause. It would be like trying to go down Monument Avenue at the Easter parade with a bunch of homo signs that said 'Christ has risen and so have we.' Good grief"—I exhaled smoke at all of them—"I can see the people in their Sunday best—the dancers, the magicians, the funnel cake makers, the Irish band, the priests, the families, the doctors, the lawyers and the rednecks and the bubbas leering and jeering at us as you try and swoop down from some modern version of the island of Lesbos. You are dead for sure, Frankie. You'll be gone before you even get started. It's Virginia, for God's sake. I can see the headlines now: Louisa County Lesbian Teacher fired over Sex in the Classroom. People would automatically think you are perverted, Bourdon. Wake up and smell the conservatives. It's all a farce. And, I'm not marching in Washington where everyone has on a rainbow hat and holds one of Brock's signs that says something like BE BOLD! FIND THE GOLD IN GAY RIGHTS FOR EVERYONE! Am I just retarded or did everyone forget that the Bible Belt begins here? Hello, is anybody in there?"

Frankie coughed a good hacker, flicked her cigarette into the ashtray, then took a large sip of her margarita.

Alma came in at us from the left. "You know, I was driving down the street the other day, Frankie, and saw a sign for the Christian Children's Fund. I wish we had one that said Gay Children's Fund." We all stared at her. "You know, just for once, a small, imaginative victory." Alma was on Frankie's side. A smile spread over Frankie's face. Now we are the Jets and Sharks.

"Well," I continued, "rainbow hats, poster board signs and pink triangles. You can count me out. There's no way in hell I can do that." I looked at them. That was it. Too damn bad. Count this librarian out, out, out.

"Vera Curran." Frankie pronounced my full name. "Do you know how to dance?"

"Frankie, we've covered this. I already told you I don't have any rhythm." I looked at Brock then to Lucy and Alma.

Lucy poked me. "Why don't you teach her how to dance, Frankie? You two would look good together." Silence fell between me and eternity and the gym teacher. I swigged my drink and looked at all of them again. The tension, suddenly, was thicker than a dark Virginia midnight in July.

For sure, now I was in trouble with these people. I got up feeling like three shits to the wind. The Tea Dance was now in full swing, and I sauntered to the bar for some relief. Resonating from the other side of the bar was a flashback of everything. All I saw were madras pants and bell bottoms and David Cassidy-in-drag posters. Big starlights flashed and flickered and took my picture in each floating second and the boom, boom, boom of the speakers were sure to send me to the planet of miracle ears by morning. Cash flowed from Elsie, beer flowed, dykes a-flowed, and everyone was seeking with glancing eyes from her to her and him to him. Big basketball women loomed over me and asked for beers. Their armpits were reminiscent of a bad night with Paula Cole. Tank tops in winter, I thought it odd. Tea Dance mentality maybe. I was sure that the average intelligence was in direct correlation to the amount of pickups which now littered the parking lot with Jeep Wranglers and old Camaros.

I talked Irish politics with the bartender. She had only one good ear, the other is nowhere to be seen—relative to Van Gogh, I mused. Even though she was missing one ear, I thought I might pick her up and go home with her. Screw Bourdon, I thought. She was out of my league, I was out of hers. This bartender liked me, I was sure. She knew geography, I learned, and didn't drive a pickup. I looked back to the table of criminals. The booth was empty.

"Hey," Frankie sidled up to me on a barstool. "Where you been you old asshole?"

"Right here, Bourdon, you old asshole." I veered around and looked at her. It was one of those drunken moments where everything was in slow motion and even though there were many distractions, I felt a still point. Reverberating like stinging icicles from the top of my head to my feet were the cells of my body. All at once they were calling me awake: *Wake up, Vera. Look at this girl before you. She has no idea, no idea you feel for her. Maybe even you don't know, but wake up.* Suffused through this was my inability to make small talk. So, I did the best I could do under the circumstances. I recited a line from my favorite poet, T.S. Eliot.

Let us go then, you and I,
When the evening is spread out against the sky.

Like a patient etherized upon a table,
Let us go through half-deserted streets,
the muttering retreats
of one night stays in cheap hotels,
Let us walk on oyster shells . . .

"Libear, are you drunk?" was all she managed. "And, if I didn't know you better, I would say that you are making a very strong pass at me." She reached for my hand. My short stubby hands reached for hers. All I could do is half-pee on myself and look over at a stupid Susan Dey poster. The blushing blood rose hard to my round, pock-marked face.

"Bourdon," I said.

"Libearian?" she said back. I squeezed her hand and let go. "Vera, good God, I believe you are blushing."

"Bourdon, I really have to tell you that—"

"Shhhhhhhh. You'll ruin the sunset."

"What sunset?"

"The one you just painted with your words for me." She said this with her eyes closed.

The cells in my body exploded. Running on a riveting steadfastness was now a body, a body hijacked by the woman of French descent before me. For a minute, I thought my nose itself might run bloody from the intensity—the nerves and my dreams and my love and my hatred for my own sexuality annealed to the walls of my heart and tried to come through my thin skin. It all felt immoral, but this girl had put her hand in mine. I would feel her anointed bits of soul-oil in my own hands reverberate for three days straight. The essence and the memory smelled as strong as a church.

She came by my house two other times that Christmas—once to give me a gift and once to ask me, again, to help her with her cause. The gift was a rainbow collar for Gracie-Mac, which I promptly shoved in the top drawer of my dresser, and even though she begged me to help her with the inclusiveness of teaching homosexuality in sex education, I respectfully declined. Nearly twenty years in the county wasn't going to be ruined by the new girl on the block, I didn't care how cute she was. Tidbits and scraps on some Bible passages would be my only criminal act toward helping her.

However, I did agree to come by her apartment for coffee the Sunday before we returned to school after break. I didn't realize that it would be a threesome as Eileen Bourdon showed up halfway through coffee and a discussion of which Indigo Girls song was the best while watching Melissa Etheridge music videos. My version of a dyke fest.

When she knocked on the door, I jumped like a spider three feet in the air. Who's that, I mouthed? My mom, Frankie mouthed. She put her fingers to her lips as I pounced from mid-air on the remote to get rid of the gyrating Etheridge on the TV screen. Too late. As I searched and scanned for the off button, I panicked and dropped it. Batteries rolled across the floor.

"Happy New Year, Mom," Frankie said as she opened the door for her.

"Happy New Year, Frankie," she stated. Her eyes fell on me then back to Frankie.

"Well, Vera," she began, "this is a nice surprise. Happy New Year to you too. A late one at that. I thought you might have joined us for Christmas dinner last week."

I eyed the batteries, then the TV, then Eileen. A new crime scene. "Oh, yes. I should have let you know that I was busy with family."

"Oh, a family girl are we?" Eileen edged the statement with a surliness I had yet encountered. Sitting in the bubba chair Frankie had bought herself for Christmas, Eileen began pulling some items from her purse. Frankie left for the kitchen to get coffee, I presumed, while Eileen began her inquisition.

"So, how long have we been working at Louisa High?" she asked, still mining the purse.

"Uh, quite a while," I said, "nearly twenty years next year." I reached for the batteries.

On the other side of Frankie's sliding glass doors, icicles clung to the edges of the balcony and a fluorescent streetlight was still illuminated. In the gray sun it brightened, and the tiny stalactites reflected weird, almost invisible, arcing waves.

"How did you and Frankie meet?" she asked, and looked about the room. Simplicity must have been Frankie's middle name because there was nothing to it. A TV in the corner sat on a simple stand. Two watercolor prints of orchids, evidently her favorite, hung above the small kitchen table located three feet from the sliding glass doors. A couch, a chair, a few magazines and one book were scattered out on the coffee table. I looked for any homo signs: pictures of women, rainbow flags, blazers haphazardly thrown over the backs of chairs, gigantic coffee mugs from Starbucks, folk music, guitars, lesbian literature. She must de-dyke before her mom comes over. Otherwise, it looked like a corporate apartment that some small-time executive would have rented for the summer.

Her question was odd. Good grief, I thought, we met at school. Faculty meetings, Fort Apache, shared students from classes. Finally, after fixing the battery quandary and shutting off the TV, I answered.

"We met at a VEA party several months ago. That was when we first began to know one another. Weirdly, our school association came second." I put the clicker down and wished secretly for Frankie to hurry.

It was a big pregnant room with an elephant in the middle.

I wanted to retreat back to my small country abode or to my pod—my Honda Civic Hatchback—and return to the planet from which, I was now assuming by Eileen's body language, I had emerged.

"Oh, you must be speaking of the VEA chapter Frankie belongs to," she paused. "It's the gay alliance one, right?"

I muttered out a yes and looked out the window. I was caught.

Eileen sat back. "My daughter is very vocal, you know. She must get it from me. Always fighting for something. Ever since she was a kid. She was the one on the block who would take up for anyone. Once, when she was in the first grade, she beat up a third-grade boy who had shoved her sister into the gravel at the bus stop. I knew then, Lord, I'm in trouble with this one. Her sister is the polar opposite, I tell you. Married. Two kids. Lovely home in the West End. Lawyer husband. But, Frankie. Frankie's another story."

I nodded, listening.

"Frankie," she went on, "yes, ma'am. A totally different story." Her lips were pursed. She got up and walked to the sliding glass doors. Eileen's body hung in the air eerily like the icicle hanging on the edge of the balcony. Her hair took on the appearance of a bad night with Phyllis Diller, I thought. *Stop it and pay attention*, I told myself.

"If you ask me, she's a very passionate woman," I stated.

"I didn't ask you," was the curt reply. Reverting to a magazine, I retreated in silence.

"Please forgive me, Vera. It's a hard time of year, and I'm a bit out of sorts. Holidays remind me of my husband and our life together. He died ten years ago, and I've spent my life trying to live up to his will and way of things. He was a Christian, you know. I guess you know what that is?" I nodded. "He was a hard-working man, and he raised his daughters to live up to the sanctity and purity of Christian values. Are you a Christian, Vera?"

"Yes, I am. But, mostly I'm just a Republican who pays taxes and seeks out what just about everyone else wants in life."

"Oh, and what is that?" she asked.

Coming in with large mugs of coffee, Frankie interrupted, "She wants what you want, Mom. A Republican president and all homos to disappear."

Eking out of my mouth was an insipid no, but no one was listening. Eileen and Frankie continued as if I was on the other side of the wall.

"Mom, it's true. Don't deny it."

"Deny what?" Eileen retorted.

"Deny that you want all homos to disappear, including me." She sipped her coffee and winked at me.

"Is she one of them?" Eileen glanced at me then back at Frankie. Another weird question popped into my head: Hadn't she seen my outfit and my hair? "I didn't want an argument, Frankie."

Frankie took on a stoic glare while a swelling juggernaut of palpable air began to swim about the room, slowly.

"It's not an argument, Mom. It's a fact of life. Two out of every twenty people like me like the same sex. It's genetic, not environmental—"

"It's a twisted choice. Don't espouse this environmental thing, young lady. You know that everything that society and the Bible tells us is that it is an abomination. If you had paid attention to your father in Sunday school instead of smoking cigarettes in the bathroom, you might know this."

"Mom"—Frankie put her hands up in the air—"why are you so angry? I mean, really. Where is the anger from? You've been mad at me since Nineteen Twelve. What's up?"

"I think I'll be going," I said. No one paid attention to me as I got up.

"Sit down, Vera," Frankie demanded.

I did.

"I'm sorry," Eileen apologized again. "This certainly isn't what I wanted to come over and do. Fight with you, dear. Here, I brought you something for the New Year." She reached for the box she had set on the table earlier. "Frankie, you know where I stand on you and your choice—"

"Mom, stop calling it a goddamned choice. They say, in fact, it's a gene you get from your mother and how a baby is bathed in the womb."

"Here," she handed Frankie the box and gathered up her things. I sat in the bleachers and continued to watch the show. "It's an angel. Why don't you try and be one for once." And with that, she stomped out the door after throwing a sneer my way. I looked down in shame.

Frankie yelled after her, "I'll be an angel if you'll canonize k.d. lang and invite her to church for Sunday school." Eileen slammed the door behind her.

"Wow! If you ask me, she's a little pissy." I looked at Frankie whose eyes welled. The ex-Navy pilot had shown me for the first time her Achilles heel. She loved and cared for her mother, what she thought of her and her life.

I finally got up from the couch. As I walked toward her, she shook her head and told me that she was all right. I stopped in the middle of the room while the juggernaut of air exhaled beneath my feet.

I was more afraid than I thought.

Frankie coughed her way into the kitchen while I gathered up to go. Later, I would remember how I thought it was then that her cancer was just beginning, metaphorically and literally.

Chapter 7

"Good morning, sleepyhead." I patted Kyle on the shoulder and head and he grumbled. "Get up and we'll take Grace for a walk. I have some information you might want to hear so you can get the story straight."

"Gay, gay, Aunt Vera," he said as he opened his eyes. "Stop trying to be straight for once, God. You dykes are always trying to swing to the other side. I want coffeeeee!" He stretched and got up. "Is Gram up yet?"

"Jesus, Mary and Joseph, is that a stupid question. She's done my laundry already and has spun cleaning dervishes around your head all morning." I walked into the kitchen to make coffee.

"Spin queen—cool." Kyle sauntered in after me.

From the far reaches of my house, my mom was folding hot towels in the laundry while she watched Fox News on the portable

TV. She'd been here often enough lately to become a permanent fixture.

"So, libear," Kyle flumped on a barstool, "what happened after she began calling you. And, you know, I didn't realize till you mentioned it that Grace has a rainbow collar on. Is it the one Frankie gave you?"

Pouring two cups, I was strangely reminded of when I had taken it out of the drawer. The day I quit as a librarian at Louisa High School. "It sure is." I patted Grace on the head and sat across from Kyle. "It's the flag of her disposition. Right, Gracie-Mac!" Wag, wag, wag. Lethal tail on that hound.

"Do you read much poetry in your English classes, Kyle?"

"Some. Uh, we have just gotten through some of the great literary moderns. Umm, like Roethke, Millay, umm, Pound, I think. Why?"

"Have you ever read anything by T.S. Eliot? The great American poet who expatriated to England because he couldn't stand America?"

"No, no Eliot as of yet." He sipped his coffee and wiped the sleepies out of his eyes.

"Well, let's see. I've taught and read great numbers of poets and about ten thousand poems. But, Eliot has something in his 'Four Quartets' that always stays with me."

"And, what's that?"

"There's a few lines about halfway into the poem, which, if you ask me, are a little long-winded. Eliot was never a terse one. Anyway, the line is about a still point."

"A still point?"

"Yeah, do you know what that is?"

"Well, if it has anything to do with sitting still, then I'm not buying it."

"No, it has nothing to do with that. Here's the line, and then I'll explain its meaning:

At the still point, there is the dance."

Kyle repeated it. "At the still point, there is the dance."

"Yes. It's such a simple line."

"Okay, libear, tell me what the interpretation is," he joked.

"Well, have you ever been somewhere or with someone and it was such a wonderful experience that it was like time was not moving forward or backward. You were just standing still, taking in all of the moments beauty—like your first kiss or high school graduation or when a parent or teacher praised you in front of others and it was significant like nothing else in the world mattered at all. Or it could be even less grand than that, like times when you were a kid playing kickball in the street or TV tag or running through sprinklers for hours with your neighborhood friends. Know what I mean?"

"I'm following you. Go on."

"Anyway, it is at those times, Eliot suggests in his line, that there is the dance, the dance of life, what we all live for but what most of us don't recognize. We are mired in the past and pulled centrifugally into the future. However, it is the small dancing moments that evade time that we need to touch like a spirit fleshed out before us. Make sense?"

"Okay, I think I might have one," Kyle said, "so, see if this is right. One time, when I was a kid, I had just learned a couple of cuss words and decided, I guess, that I was going to use them whenever I felt like it. So, we were playing whiffle ball in Marianne Kennelly's backyard. Mom was pitching the ball to me for the billionth time while I was hovering over dad's penny loafer as home plate. Everyone was sitting down in the outfield because, in my words, 'I can't hit the damn ball.' I must have been five or six. So, after a billion and one pitches, I say that I'm goddamned mad at everyone. I stomp home, pack my stuffed animals and all the underwear you can imagine and run away to the big rocks down by the creek. I can remember thinking that they shouldn't get all riled up because I can't hit a whiffle ball, and they'll see how special I am now that I've run away and am going to live with the rock people. Looking back now, it was hysterical."

"That's right," I said, "that moment stays with you. Do you have another one?"

"Aunt Vera. I can't tell you the big one."

"Oh, God. Yes, please leave that one out."

"So, when did you know about your, you know . . ." He paused.

"My sexuality?"

"Yeah."

"I think I was fourteen and in love with Chris Evert."

"Chris Evert. She's pretty cute for an old girl. When did you tell Gram?"

"I was seventeen. The guilty Catholic girl. Keeping secrets had always been a bit tricky for me. But, I felt she should know because she had always taught me the virtue of telling the truth. They instill it in you, you know, the Catholics, at a young age. No bad thoughts, tell the truth, forgive everyone but yourself. Anyway, one night she and I had watched some movie on TV that had a gay character. I forget what it was, but she liked it. It was my small signal of hope. After the movie, I sat down in our big rocker in front of her and told her I was pretty sure I was gay."

"Oh, God. Did Gram freak?"

"Well, at first she was fine. Then about halfway into the discussion, she asked for valium, whiskey and the phone."

"The phone?"

"She wanted to call my sister at college and tell her I was in trouble. I thought she might interrupt her making her pot brownies for her sorority sisters, but Mom thought it would make me straight if the whole family knew right away, and the news would perhaps embarrass me into forgetting about the whole idea. Then she fainted."

"Gram fainted?"

"Yep, I was up until four in the morning making her breathe into a paper bag in between whiskey drinks. Gram's a teetotaler, you know."

"What?"

"She doesn't drink."

Just then, Momma appeared in the kitchen. She pulled out bacon and made preparations to begin breakfast. "What are you all talking about?" she asked.

"Still points," Kyle replied.

"Still points?"

"Yeah, Momma. Big long story." I winked at Kyle. "We're taking Grace for a walk. Want to go?"

"Now, why would you think I would want to take that slobbering, giant furball anywhere, Vera?"

"Mom?"

"What?" she said, exasperated.

"I love you."

"Oh, be quiet and you two get out of here."

I painted God once in Sunday school when I was four years old. An old man with a long beard. He was my rendition of what the celestial heavens were supposed to be. It wasn't so celestial except that his head was really large with a huge face that took up most of the drawing. A two-inch thick blue line covered the top of the paper right behind his magnanimous head—the sky. The ground below was splotched with brown and green. God didn't have any arms. Most of the pictures I drew at that age had armless people. As an educator, I would learn later in life that it meant I was asking for help or my family needed help. I think I left the arms off because I wasn't much good at drawing them. God with big beards and thick blue lines were my best. I just wasn't an arm girl.

Kyle grabbed his hat and we were off to the wood path beyond my deck. I told him more of what happened with Frankie after Christmas break and the bad cup of coffee we had shared with her mother. I relented to her wishes about the Bible and its throat-hold on homosexuals and tried to give her as much information as possible while she researched the need to have the gay curriculum added. But, that was it. Insistent on staying on the sidelines, I watched her take on the Bible Belt the last six months she taught at Louisa High School. She attended all of the VEA meetings and outlined a plan to take to the school board as a possible resolution to adopt into the Virginia teaching codes. The more she tried to do this, the more saddened I became watching her get thrown overboard.

News traveled quickly in Louisa County and by the end of February, even though Frankie never once admitted to her own lesbianism, the rumor-mill started. I didn't know that by May, Frankie would be getting sick with cancer. I also didn't know that by March of the following year I would be her wife.

"You two got married?" Kyle stopped me, incredulous.

"Oh, Kyle, hell no. In the state of Virginia? You know it can't happen and won't for a million years."

"Well, you said you got married, libear!" he ribbed me.

"Not in the way you understand it."

"Well, what then?"

"That's a secret, young man."

"Hey, you told me that you don't keep secrets!"

"No, I told you that keeping secrets was tricky sometimes."

"Come on, Aunt Vera," he pleaded, "pleeeeeease?" He turned his hat around so that the adjuster band faced me and the sun. He made me laugh when he got down on one knee.

"Okay, goofy." We continued down the path which picked up a small brook near a walking bridge leading to a field of neighboring horses. Grace meandered ahead of us, sniffing, trotting and wagging her tail.

Finally, I began. "Well, we didn't get married in a church, Kyle. Maybe I should start with how we first got together."

He nodded his head.

"The summer after her first and last year at Louisa High, she was going through her first round of chemo. They diagnosed her with stage-three lung cancer. Funny, it wasn't from the smoking. They traced it to exposure she had to chemicals during her Navy tenure."

"Why did she leave the Navy, anyway?" Kyle interrupted.

"Don't ask, don't tell. It ruined her."

"Oh."

"Plus, she had always wanted to try teaching. She loved kids. Much more than I ever did."

Kyle threw a stick for Grace. "Aunt Vera, you love kids."

"Well, I know I love you. You know, maybe I need to back up and tell you a few things before I get into the whole cancer, marriage, Key West thing."

"Key West? You didn't tell me about Key West."

"Frankie's favorite place in the world. We went twice in ninety-nine—once with Alma, Brock and Lucy."

"Oh, no," Kyle said, punctuating it with a hand over his mouth.

"Oh, yes," I nodded. "And, we went once by ourselves. The Freedom Fest for Women. Late October."

"Sounds like a blast. Tell me."

"Wait a minute, hold onto your adjuster band. Let me first tell you what happened between Frankie and the school board and Louisa High before I get into the fun stuff."

"God, I bet that was a crazy time."

"Yep. So, the Post-it notes kept coming with *what do women do*? I kept returning notes telling her that women *run, hide, get out of Dodge*—any appropriate verb I could find to tell her to stop the insanity. But, it was all to no avail. She wanted to start a movement. And I basically stayed on the sidelines like I had always done. Homosexuality discussions scared me, and I was full of shame in my bones. It's like the shame leaked out of them and into my skin. I didn't think any of it was right. Keep the homo agenda quiet and everyone stays happy."

"Don't tell?" Kyle muttered rhetorically.

"Yeah, don't tell. It was a great way to live, I thought. Part of me, however, felt a great draw to her because she was so strong and didn't really care about what might stand in her way. So, I gave her some Bible insight on Post-it notes and at Apache. And she charged on. One day in February of that year, I went to the school board meeting and sat in the back. News had gotten out about it through Maggie Winterfield. She told her dad about what was going on, and he advised Eileen Bourdon on how to go to bat for the school district. Brock and Alma and Lucy showed up to support Frankie. I almost didn't go on the big debate day. But, I managed to go anyway. Something in me said I should go, regardless of how much shame I felt."

"So, you went. What happened?"

"They smashed her."

"They did?"

"Yep, but funny thing. If you ask me, Frankie thought she had won."

"How?"

"By the way she smiled at me exiting the James Monroe Building."

I was not sure the order of how things happened. My tenses were all shifty, blurring my vision.

The James Monroe Building near the center of town was where they held the local school board meetings once a month. It was a single story building and the central meeting room looked like the vestibule of a church. On the wall to the right as one walked in hung the Ten Commandments which had spouted out loud and clear for more than seventy years. The simplicity of the stony building reflected the simplicity of the townspeople. The grass around the brick and the sidewalk was clipped just so. Dogwoods and azaleas decorated the perimeter of the building and out front on this day was Eileen's prayer group—Holt Meyers, Maggie Winterfield and the rest, praying the Lord's Prayer in a singsong way over and over again. The state flag, the American flag and the Louisa County flag flapped in the wind to the cadence of the prayer. The state flag's motto is *Sic Semper Tyranis*: Thus always to tyrants. I reflected on this double entendre and walked into the building to sit in the back of the galleries on that late February day. It was 72 degrees outside—a Virginia chinook, the most fickle weather in the world. Sitting in the back, I saw a small spider crawling slowly under the chair in front of me. It did not scare me. It was too small.

There were five members of the school board—four men and one woman, Eileen Bourdon. Robert Patterson was the president-in-charge until they hired a new one. A recent scandal had found the former president sleeping with a schoolteacher from Montgomery County who had also embezzled money from every local charity around. To date, he was still on the lam. Patterson was a young, clean-cut looking man who wore the latest in men's clothing—Mr. GQ himself. Must have gotten in on his looks, I thought. John Russell was the fattest, sloppiest looking man I'd ever laid eyes on. He wore a fat tie that was three inches too short, and his bottom button was unbuttoned so his stomach could relieve itself out. White-gray hair was unusually long over his ears, and he was balding on the top. His best known contributions to the town were the big tips he left at the local bar each night of the week. It kept the bar in business for most of the year. Word had it that he had beaten his wife on more than one occasion but, like most women, she kept praying and kept quiet. Louisa County hadn't gotten past the fifties. It was easy to tell. Douglas Bliley was the town's funeral director and made it to most of the school board meetings unless he was bringing in a body. His family had buried three-fourths of the town over the last fifty years. Bliley was a stodgy man who, as he sat down, pulled a Bible from his briefcase. He opened it and thumbed through some passages earmarked by his own Post-its. The fourth and final member was Mr. Pinhead himself: Jake Neidermeyer. Anyone with the name Neidermeyer always had acne and greasy hair. He was no different.

The meeting began with the usual: the invocation, the Pledge of Allegiance, the approval of the minutes, the agenda, ad nauseum. When they finally got down to business, they discussed the big issues—which elementary school got what kind of funding, how much control was going to be needed at the middle school for disadvantaged youth. Parents from all over sent their kids to Louisa's alternative middle school.

While this was all taking place, I sat to the left side where Frankie and her VEA advisor could not see me. She never looked behind her. She fiddled some papers, and her mother, who came in late, sat down and ignored her. I had called Brock, but he hadn't arrived yet. I had wished he were here. As the meeting progressed, I decided to take a break and have a smoke. Bliley and Russell were having much indecision over relocating graduation to a different venue, so much so that I thought we would relocate right into the next millennium and not notice. My eyes were heavy.

Thank God I went out. Brock Goldberg was leaning on the back of Frankie's truck three sheets to the wind and wearing a baseball cap emblazoned with a rainbow. This must be our small demonstration, I thought. Just Brock and me.

"Been in?" he asked as he stumped out a cigarette and shoved his hands in his pockets.

"Yes. I'm not so sure about this, Brock." Alma and Lucy drove up in Alma's clunker. We both waved. "I mean she shouldn't be doing this. Now you may think I'm an outsider—"

"Yep." He reached inside the truck for another beer. Some of the prayer kids by the flagpole recognized me and started my way, waving. Shit. It was Marty Hanna, Mr. Romeo himself, and some of his girlie entourage.

"You don't understand, Vera. She's on a mission. And, you know how it goes—'To lift someone up, you must be on higher ground.' What subterranean ground are you on, Veer?" Stung, I didn't answer.

"She's been on this mission as long as I've known her. She can't wrap her brain around why we peeps"—he pointed to his cap—"can't get the equality we deserve."

"Brock, you two need your heads examined. They are going to eat her alive in there. By the time they are finished with the theatre of the gay agenda, the record will be complete for everyone to see and read, and she will no longer be employed by Louisa County."

"Is that what you think, Veer? Are you really that uptight in your conservative ass that you think they would fire her for being who she is?" He swigged another swallow. Lucy and Alma were stalled with Lucy fixing her makeup.

"Brock, wake up. If you ask me, they aren't going to fire her for who she is, they are going to fire her for who she isn't. That's the kicker. They'll make it up. They'll make it up like people have always done to get people out of the way. They'll falsify documents saying she left the room while administering SOL tests, or maybe they will pull her mail, and she'll fail to turn in important items to the principal. Or whatever—they can do it as easy as that. Or, maybe they'll say she's been staring at the girls in the locker room while they were getting dressed. Jesus, I don't know!"

Marty Hanna picked up Holt Meyers as they moved toward us. My stomach clenched.

Brock put his hand on my shoulder. "Vera, why are you so worried about her job?"

"Because, she's my friend, and I'm in love with her. I don't want her to go. It's why I go to work everyday—to see her, to send her notes, to smoke with her, to watch her." There. I said it out loud. I stepped away from his hand and felt my lips quivering.

"Howdy, ho, ho, hosebags," Lucy barked as she and Alma approached. Alma pushed her glasses up with her middle finger and hugged Brock.

"Have you two been in the meeting?" Alma released Brock and looked at me.

"Hey, M-M-Miss Curran!" It was Holt, lisp, stutter and all. Super.

"Hey, Holt. How are you? Hey, Marty. How's the play going?" He shrugged his shoulders. "What are you two doing up here? These are my friends—Brock, Alma and Lucy. Guys, this is Marty Hanna and Holt Meyers—Mr. Romeo and Mr. Wrestler."

Holt started and we strained through his lisp. "Everyone down at school knows about the agenda. So we decided to come up and say a prayer or two. Big stuff for our county, huh, Miss Curran?" He asked and I shrugged my shoulders. Eileen must have told her prayer group, I thought.

"It's so nice to meet you two," Brock extended his hand.

"Nice to meet you, too," Holt extended his. "S-S-So, how do you all know each other?"

Brock heaved up his chest like a bull and then said in his faggiest of fag manner, "We met at a gay pride festival for teachers." He said it, threw his hat down at my feet and marched inside.

"Really?" Holt looked at me then to Alma and Lucy. Marty waved to Maggie's father coming in from his vehicle. The Baptist preacher from Eileen's church.

I stood frozen, cataleptic.

Lucy poked me, and I awakened to saying, "No, Holt. It's not true. You know I'm just an old librarian who doesn't do much of anything." It was the stupidest comment I could manage.

They just stared at me, bewildered. I was sure they all knew I was a dyke in librarian's clothing or maybe I was a librarian in dyke's clothing. I don't know. I was mixed up and mixing up my metaphors.

"Okay," Alma said. "Can we go in now to see Frankie?" She cemented the reason we were all there. Alma was always giving things away. A big zit was surfacing on the middle of her forehead. Wishing for a bobby pin was my only sane thought.

Back inside, Alma and Lucy and I sat behind Brock. Except for the school board, Frankie, Eileen's prayer group and Maggie's dad, the room held only a smattering of principals and teachers with other agendas, I was sure. Confusing thoughts rushed through my head. I tried to remember the four big issues I had discussed with Frankie—Sodom, Leviticus, the New Testament list of sins and Paul's Letters to the Romans. Jesus said nothing of the whole homo matter. The ol' hippie just wanted people to love one another and forgive, from what I could siphon out. We were to imitate Jesus and his humility. This was it. The truth. The only truth was the implication made by the son of God. If it had been such a huge sin, he would have addressed it.

I was more confused than I had ever thought.

With my head in full spin, I landed right back in another childhood image. Something made me go there. It was moving around inside of me, hard and strong. Transferring from Holden Caulfield's hat was me—a child. Lost and alone, I galloped on my play horse through Sherwood Forest, right behind the cul-de-sac and the neighborhood creek. Trotting and cantering, I went by the two large rocks near the water where an old broken drawbridge lay. My mother was screaming my name—*Veraaaa, Veraaaa.* I ignored her and broke into a run through the foggy marsh on the north side of the bridge, directionless, slapping trunks of trees, stinging my hands. *Veraaa, Veraaa, where are you? Come home, come home.* I am the ugly gargoyle, the Hunchback of Notre Dame, the Beast. Mute and deaf, I continued galloping, running. The foggy spirit rushes into my lungs. Full, I fall down. Centrifugal cobalt sky in a semi-circle from horizon to horizon covers me. *VERA, COME HOME.*

I was my own anagram.

Today, in this room I was still lost, however, something in me bloomed differently. From the caverns of my own small ribs, my own small frame was my heart, striking its billionth beat, allowing my blood to and from the vestibule of my soul. I began to see fortune in front of me and began, without prior knowledge, to give in to it.

I still felt my mother screaming for me. But now, this woman, Eileen Bourdon, sat silently screaming in the dark gallows ahead. Surrounding me was a strange room, heightened by what Frankie had said was true—smart people who made bad decisions based on the Bible, which half didn't even read. Education's biggest enemy was the separation of church and state and the buffoons who couldn't see the difference.

Eileen Bourdon stood up and smoothed her skirt. Hair higher than usual, she picked at it with her hands, checked her painted nails and sat back down. She was the official speaker of the school board. Maggie's father sat on the right side at the front across the aisle from Frankie, the prayer group in the corresponding row behind him.

She spoke. "Now that the official business of the board is complete," Patterson said. He coughed and fixed his tie, lengthening his hand down the front like a long phallus. She paused, "now that the official business of the board is complete, we will now open—"

Brock hacked out a cough that echoed like a sonic boom. Everyone looked back. The echo stopped, and she began again.

"We," she eyed Brock, "can now open the floor to new business and public comment." She looked to Russell who was nodding off. Neidermeyer had his finger in his ear. Examining the contents was of most interest. Bliley looked intent on Frankie and scrunched his lips and nose together.

In the middle of the floor, just in front of the board, was a podium and a microphone. Picking up her notes packed in a leather folio, Frankie approached the bench. Stunningly beautiful. She was stunningly beautiful. Black, all black. A new suit from Nordstrom's where she and her mother always shopped for special occasions. Alma grabbed Lucy's hand and mine.

Lucy whispered, "Come on, Frankie." Eyeing Eileen, Lucy began to say "ho, ho" something till Alma smacked her on the back of the head.

Frankie settled her notes and put a Post-it on the tip top of the podium. What it said, I didn't know, but she fingered it for a second, smoothing it over.

"My name is Frankie Bourdon, and I teach at Loui—"

"Uh, Ms. Bourdon," Eileen interrupted, "the board is aware of where you teach and each has your proposal for a resolution in hand." She held it up for all to see. "Let's just get to your public comment, please."

Brock looked back. "Bitchus interruptus!" I put my hands to my mouth. He mouthed "bite my ass."

Frankie ignored Eileen and continued.

"I am a teacher at Louisa High School. And, as both a student and now an educator in the state of Virginia, I would like to comment on and make necessary changes to what the state's family life curriculum dictates to us on what to teach in the health classroom. I, like other health and PE teachers in my department, gladly embrace what is set before us. We teach about physical, mental and sexual health. We teach about families and family life. We teach about fostering healthy relationships with family, peers and figures of authority. We also teach diversity. Generally speaking, we teach about ethnicity and diversity in different religions and social hierarchies. This is also true in our English and history classes where diversity is the common thread in the fabric of our multicultural curriculum. We teach young people about the kinds of relationships at all levels. We expose them to the triumph and struggles through literature and real life stories, but where do we, I ask, teach about homosexuality? Do we even speak the word? Do we really need to discuss it, some may ask? Where does the whole idea and lifestyle of homosexuality come from? Where are the roots of it and why are there nearly thirty million people in America living its lifestyle? Is it a choice? Is it environmental? Is it genetic? Where does one find out? Where does the search begin? If I have these feelings, is it wrong or am I okay?

"Today, in 1999, even educators in our county are taught and trained on diversity and different ethnicities. However, as a sidenote, and like the students I teach, nowhere is there anything—not one thing—written about how to deal with the diversity of homosexuality. In this state, and especially in this county like many others, we can only discuss homosexuality if a student asks a question about it. That's it. We can only discuss it *if* a student asks a question about it. This is the one and only recourse homosexuals have in the school system. Now, I ask you. What child is going to bring it up? What child?

"Children need to know about this minority which has been ridiculed and marginalized for hundreds, even thousands of years. It needs to be taught for their safety, their health and to save lives of the countless ones who are lost every year.

"We expose our youth to writings of great homosexual writers like Whitman, Melville, Dickinson. Yet, we never once discuss their sexuality. Even the greatest writers are pushed into the hall of shame because many in education don't want to deal with the touchy subject.

"Until mainstream America begins to acknowledge and even herald the contributions of gay people everywhere, until we put gay people on the same scale as heterosexual people, until we can teach the diversity of sexual orientation in the classroom in counties like Louisa, then homosexuality will continue to be relegated to the margins and dismissed. We will continue, like we have since the black cloud of shame and ignorance enveloped us, to lose our children, our good children to moral reprehension, bullying, physical beating, substance abuse, shame, depression and the worst—suicide and murder.

"The Civil Rights movement is the completion of the full circle which put an ending exclamation mark to the pervasive inequality between blacks and whites. Albeit, the story of the struggle does not end there. It was a battle built on strife and struggle which is very similar to what our young gay children face today—the only contrast is the color of skin, a genetic predisposition that no one can change. The same genetic predisposition that charges the cells of one's body to want to be close to someone of the same sex: spiritually, physically, familially and lovingly. Just like black people cannot wipe away the color of their skin, neither can gay people wipe away the genetic fluid of the cells that make them who they are. It simply runs too deep.

"It is time for counties like Louisa to wake up and fully expose the youth to this life that is sewn into the fabric of this country and world. If homosexuality continues to be punctuated and stopped by social intolerance, biblical allusions and shame, and tossed aside as insignificant because of those stigmas and not included in the classroom as it should, it won't until then, come full circle in doing what it should intend to do—give homosexuality a voice, align and treat heterosexuality and homosexuality as inclusive proclivities not as opposing entities and give hope to the millions of gay youth who battle with their identities as if they are the only ones in the world who feel the way they feel.

"I am here to ask you, the local school board to consider adopting my proposal and making it a resolution as a commitment to changing the curriculum for the young people we need to save. It is my obligation. And, frankly, I hope that you will see and understand that it is yours, too."

I was stunned by her poise and choice of words. Brock turned around and looked at Alma and Luce and me. At once we all high-fived. Even me.

There was a pause in the room as the board took notes and shuffled some papers.

Finally, Eileen spoke. "Thank you, Ms. Bourdon. Is that your statement in full?" Frankie nodded. "Then you may sit down. Is there anyone here who would like to speak for or against this proposal?"

Maggie Winterfield's dad raised his hand.

"Yes, Mr. Winterfield. You may approach the podium." She smiled at him. Bliley continued writing his notes while the others looked bored. Russell was almost snoring.

He had only the Bible in his hand. Come on, Frankie.

"Mr. Patterson, Mr. Russell (he opened his eyes), Mr. Bliley, Mr. Neidermeyer and Mrs. Bourdon. My name is Paul Winterfield and I have a daughter who is a student at Louisa High School. Her name is Maggie. She's an honor roll student, a cheerleader and a flutist in the marching band. Yet all of this is shadowed by what her great membership is in life—she's a Christian prayer leader in her school youth group. Early on, she accepted Jesus Christ as her savior, and my wife and I have done our best to make sure she grows up in a loving, warm and giving home. We attend all of her school functions and as a family, we are, as the community knows, very involved in the first Baptist Church in Richmond. I am the preacher there, and Maggie and my wife attend services there to support me and their faith.

"Ms. Bourdon," he turned to Frankie, "I believe you teach her boyfriend, Holt Meyers. He's here today." He turned and pointed to Holt. Holt put his hand up. "He and Maggie have been going together for several years, and he also is a member of the school's prayer group as well as an active member in my church. Brilliant and caring and supportive young man. A young man and a young woman—good citizens. Both attend Louisa County High where both my wife and I attended more than twenty years ago.

"Now, it is my understanding—let me echo your words—that you want to include the teaching of homosexuality in the family life curriculum at Louisa?" He waited for Frankie to nod.

"Well, now you talk about great writers and, let's see, thirty million people sharing in the same lifestyle. You talk about choice and genetics. Now, hmmm. We are looking straight into the gun of evolution and creationism: the dueling paradigms that have soiled American education for over eighty years. I, if you will, am making a parallel. Heterosexuality on the same playing field as homosexuality? Hmmm. So, we have roughly two hundred and sixty million people in the United States, and you say that thirty million are homosexual. Well, first of all, I'd like to see where you did your research, young lady. If we want to put them on an equal playing field, then it looks like we will need some more homosexual recruits since heterosexuals outnumber homosexuals by your estimation of nearly two hundred and thirty million people.

"Well, I don't know about you, but I'd rather my daughter to continue to share in the same education as we've always had at Louisa—less any inclusiveness that you speak of. My Bible, Ms. Bourdon"—he looked at Eileen who nodded her head—"appears to have stayed the same over a few thousand or more years. My Old Testament sitting nicely next to my New Testament. Both of which testify to the truth of what is morally right and what is morally wrong. And I hate to be the bearer of bad news, but homosexuality has never been on the same playing ground as heterosexuality. Nowhere in the Bible does it condemn my way of life, but homosexuals, gays as you may say it, are a whole other beast. More than ten times we see how it is an immoral act which soils everyone it touches. From Sodom to Psalms to Paul, it's all here"—he tapped on his Bible—"and we simply can't change what has and will be till kingdom come, now can we?

"We know that homosexual behavior is wrong and that people who act on their attraction to the same sex, even in loving and faithful relationships, are committing a sin against nature and against God. I mean whole cities were destroyed for the abomination, people were blinded. Paul says that homosexual acts were symptoms of people refusing to acknowledge God. Does that not sound like a choice to you? Refusing is a choice, not something ingrained in your mitochondria. You simply can't be one with Christ if you engage in this kind of behavior. And frankly, Ms. Bourdon"—he turned to Frankie—"I don't want my daughter and her boyfriend and any students at Louisa exposed to what is not supposed to be.

"This book has been the benchmark for human beings for what is right and wrong. And, this school board, Eileen, has the obligation to continue to educate young people in the right way, not the wrong one. It is your duty to uphold this code of ethics, this natural way of life: heterosexuality, a man with a woman. Including the teaching of homosexual life will destroy the seeds of morality and shake the foundation of which we Christians work for day by day, week by week, and year by year to keep our children safe, moral and strong.

"For God's sake and our children, do your duty and keep this woman and her ideas out of our curriculum, out of our classrooms, and out of our children's lives. Thank you."

Mr. Winterfield held up his Bible and took his seat. Like Channel Five, he had flubbed out his boondoggle.

Eileen Bourdon looked to her cohorts and then addressed the audience again.

"If anyone would like to speak further on this subject, then the floor is open at the podium. Please step forward if you wish."

Frankie rose to rebut but was interrupted again by her mother.

"Uh, Ms. Bourdon, we've heard your statement already. Please be open to letting someone else speak."

Lucy whispered, "Be open! Is she insane?"

"Shush," Alma hit her with her elbow. "Wait and see what happens, goofy."

"Don't call me goofy, geeky!" Lucy said.

There was a moment's pause till Russell spoke up.

"Is there any other business, then?" He wiped his nose and rubbed his eyes.

"Patterson, do you have any other business?" Patterson shook his head. "Jake?" Another shake of the head. "Well, Mrs. Bourdon, I think it's time to wrap things up so I can get home to the wife."

Frankie stood up. "If I may, Mrs. Bourdon and members of the school board, I would like to respond to Mr. Winterfield."

"Ms. Bourdon, I believe you have had enough of a say. We will let you know at the next board meeting if, in fact, we feel an adoption of your proposal to a resolution is necessary. It will be our first order of business. Now, if you'll take your seat, I—"

"No, I will not take my seat, Mrs. Eileen Bourdon. I want to rebut what Mr. Winterfield said. Please give me a minute to talk."

"We already feel as if you have said quite enough, Ms. Bourdon. You had your time, now please—"

Frankie ignored her.

"Mr. Winterfield and members of the board," she approached the podium again and placed the same Post-it just on the upper edge. It was the only thing in her hand. "Mr. Winterfield uses the Bible to condemn homosexuality, right? Well, let me tell you that we all know and should know like Mr. Winterfield himself that the Bible does many things to condemn all sorts of behavior. Let's see. In Leviticus, if one reads further, it also prohibits intercourse with a woman during her period, the crossbreeding of animals, sowing fields with two kinds of seed, wearing garments made of different materials, marrying a divorced woman, tattoos, cursing your father or your mother, eating meat with blood still on it, stealing, lying, adultery, witchcraft and prostitution, to name a few.

"Like the Sodom story, Leviticus is used to taint homosexuality, however Sodom is not about homosexuality, it is about the attempted same-sex gang rape of Lot's guests. The immorality is not about the sexuality, it is about the rape. Raping women or men is equally wrong. However, once in use that it was about homosexuality, once it came about, it has stayed about the wrong idea.

"Now, please, I'm not the Bible expert, however, I do know one thing. Jesus, who I believe Mr. Winterfield and I both agree is our savior, says not one thing either for or against homosexuality. If it were indeed such a vile sin to be shunned and shamed, don't you think he would have given it even a little lip service?" She was using my points.

"That's enough, Ms. Bourdon," Eileen Bourdon stood up. "You have crossed the line."

"No, Mom. I believe you and Mr. Winterfield have."

"That's enough between you two," John Russell stepped in. "This is a no-win situation Ms. Bourdon. I feel that it will probably be the decision of this local school board to keep things the way they have been—"

"Yes, Mr. Russell," Eileen interrupted him, "you are correct.

I am in full concordance to what Mr. Winterfield has said here today. Our school system should stay as it is and teach family life the way our society has always done so—with dignity, with fortitude and with the highest of morality. It is the way our founding fathers would have wanted it, and the way, as Mr. Winterfield so eloquently stated, the way our Lord and Bible says is the right thing to do. Our children should never be tainted in any way. Drugs and alcohol are hard enough burdens to bear without bringing in the idea that homosexuality is okay. It is indeed an abomination and abhorrent behavior.

"Now, Ms. Bourdon. You are my daughter. And, you know I love you. But this has got to stop for your sake and for the children you teach. It's just not right, Frankie."

"No, Mom," Frankie interjected, "it isn't right. This isn't right. But, imagine this. If you and the rest of the people in this room close your eyes for just a minute and think about this. There is a young man in Alabama who is blond and handsome. Imagine he is your son, just for a moment. He wakes up one morning like he always does and gets dressed in his Old Navy jeans and a Polo shirt and drives his mother's Grand Prix to school. He gets to homeroom and tells his friend that he told his folks over the weekend that he's gay. Then, after the Pledge of Allegiance and moment of silence, he walks down the hallway in front of the office, past guidance, and past his ninth grade English teacher who taught him about Shakespeare and love and tumult. He goes into the boys' bathroom, looks in the mirror and, even though he has a scholarship to go to Tulane University and study biology, he realizes that his one out has become his only avenue in—death. He takes his shirt off, cuts his wrists, writes 'I'm sorry' on the bathroom mirror, walks into the stall behind him and puts his slit wrists in the toilet and flushes his own blood down the drain till he passes out and dies.

Meantime, Mr. Connor down the hall fields a question about some queer on TV and dismisses it because he doesn't care about fags. All the while the young blond boy from Alabama watches his own blood go down the drain. Imagine, just for a second, it's here, he's here, it's Virginia and the son is yours. Would an open, clear discussion of his sadistic morality have saved his life? Or, would an open, clear discussion about the Bible and Jesus's view have saved him? Who do you trust? You, the modern day judges, or Jesus? Or, the people who talked around him? Who do you want saved? Yourself? Or, the young man in the bathroom? I, in turn, hope your egos aren't that hijacked by your own misinterpretations about the Bible and what's right and wrong. Thank you. God bless you and this school board to make the right decision."

She tore the Post-it note off of the podium and sat down.

Within ten minutes, the whole thing was over. The school board thanked everyone for being there and the session was dismissed into a closed session. Frankie would know the outcome in four weeks. Four weeks.

Just in time for spring break.

Just in time for our first trip to Key West.

As Frankie and the VEA rep exited the building she looked at us all sitting in the back. Like her, we knew, too, what the outcome would be. But, Frankie was trying. Trying to make her small mark, trying to make her small movement. She wanted a story for the millennium March on Washington and this was one of her baby steps to it.

As she walked by us, we all half-waved at her.

When Frankie looked at me, my stomach dropped. Her strong hand held the one Post-it note in her hand. She turned it toward me, her Bible tutor and word coach, and smiled with her cobalt blues and mouthed what it said: *What do women do*?

And with that she marched out the back door. Alma said something about going home to bake a pie. Brock apologized for being snippy with me. Lucy walked out to catch Frankie for a ride to Freddy's for one of Elsie's margaritas.

I sat for a minute. The darkness outside harbored the strange stars of the night that were emanating white waving spirits from their own auras. Frankie Bourdon was becoming my strange epiphany—the hardening of my blood from years of soulless searching seemed to expire from my own hundred-year-old battle with self-esteem.

Instead of me following me, it was then that I agreed with myself to follow her.

Chapter 8

Kyle sat back and listened to more . . .

Duvall Street in Key West in March was crawling with the gayness of the gay people. It was a GLBT paradise like none of us had ever seen—me, included. I had traveled out of Louisa twice: Once to go to the beach and once to Columbus, Ohio, but only for family vacations. This street, the main artery into the historic town that had housed Hemingway and a litany of others, was a Mecca and manna from heaven had opened up and showered it with rainbow eclectic and blue and gold. The freedom was palpable with the colorful flags lining the sidewalks, symbolic of everyone's disposition, even mine.

Alma, Lucy, Brock and Frankie and I had coordinated the trip by following Elsie down with her flag football ensemble to celebrate spring break and Frankie's "victory" loss over the Louisa school board. She called it that because even though she was struck down by the school board, four-zip, she knew that it was now public record and that her voice had been heard. She told me that was what she was all about. She just wanted to be heard, heard, heard.

"Oh, Lord," Brock said as we sauntered down to the west side of Duvall, "make me an instrument of your phallic peace. I've never seen so many beautiful men. Frankie, bite my gay ass. Whenever you need a trip after talking to school hags, then count me in. My nursing skills are going to come in handy here. I'm going to fluff pillows and do all kinds of bed checks."

Alma and Lucy walked ahead while Brock and Frankie walked behind me. I was in the middle, tugging at my shirt and loving every minute of the street vendors and musicians, soaking in the sun and the March heat. Every few steps, the palm trees protruded and waved their leafy bodies over us, sheltering only our shadows from the sun.

"Brock, we aren't going to see much of you are we?" Frankie joked.

"Nor of me!" Lucy yelled back. "Alma's going to go to the Hemingway museum while I go to the nearest strip club. Any takers?"

"Vera wants to go," Alma stated, "she hasn't seen a naked woman since 1883."

Frankie tapped me on the shoulder, "Libear! Don't tell me you've been holding out?" she jested.

I stopped and responded. "Alma is lying. I saw her saggy breasts at Lucy's house last year. Since then I've decided to become asexual. Thanks, Alm."

"You're welcome."

"Sex is overrated, anyway," I said.

"Oh, really?" Frankie asked. "How is that so?"

Lucy stopped me. "Vera says you should only have it when the spirit moves you. Well, I don't know about your spirit, Veer, but I have to have a sexual movement more than once every ten years or so."

"Vera, don't let patience prevail," Brock quoted. "You must be ready to pop like a blister?"

"I'd say her whole body is a blister." Alma looked at me, pushed up her glasses. I mocked her and stuck out my tongue. She stuck hers out back.

"If you're not going to use it, you two, then keep it behind your teeth," Lucy laughed.

"Here it is," Frankie said, pointing to the Sunset Grille.

"Wow, more gay people. Someone pinch my ass." Frankie did.

"Ow, Jesus," I barked at her. She slapped me in the back of the head.

"Good God, libear! You have been on a dry spell. We're going to have to see if we can get you some action while we're here. Brock, are you on it?" Frankie asked.

"Like white on rice," Brock answered.

"Like flannel on dykes," I joked.

"Like lipstick on lesbians," Lucy honed in.

"Like ink on paper," Alma said. We all looked at each other, rolled our eyes, then just stared at her.

"Okay, boys. Let's meet some people." Brock walked onto the outdoor decking where a gazebo bar jutted out to the side. Bamboo covered the awning where three bartenders worked its circular cove. We were on top of the Gulf of Mexico, green waves lapping against the pylons.

Louisa County was a foreign country by now.

We found a large table by the edge of the deck. It was Frankie's lifelong dream to watch the sunset on the west coast of

Key West, and since it was her victory trip and all, it was her call to go there. So, there we were, drinking margaritas and her and Brock trying to find me a hookup when the only one I wanted to hook up with was the French criminal sitting right next to me.

After retrieving the 'ritas, Elsie Miser and a group of her football cronies spotted us from the corner of the large deck and approached.

"Hey, girls and boy," Elsie was holding the hand of a young girl, the one who got her fired at Louisa. "What's up. It's good to see that someone else is serving you margaritas instead of me. Did you guys hear about the big concert tonight?"

"What concert?" we all asked at once.

"The Indigo Girls are playing on one of the cruise ships. We're all going on board and crash it."

"Haven't you heard, Elsie?" Lucy asked. "We are the Indigo Girls. You know, Nomads, Indians, Saints. Alma is the Nomad. Frankie is the Indian. And Vera is the Saint."

"Who's Melissa Etheridge?" Elsie asked.

"Brock. He wants a boy to bring him some water," Lucy said. We all high-fived, then Alma asked why she was the Nomad. Lucy told her it was because she was always all over the place and that no one knew where she was coming from.

"Hey," Frankie interjected, "why is Vera the Saint?"

I spoke up. "Because I'm anointed with these two cherubs." I pointed to Luce and Alm.

"Anointed," Frankie said, "what does anoint mean exactly, libear?"

"Well, it has something to do with oil, I believe, and consecration."

"Owall, oil?" Elsie said, "has anyone ever told you, Vera, that you sound like Jethro when you talk?"

"I prefer Ellie May," I said.

"Oil—Ellie May!" Lucy smacked me on the head. "You're one to talk about oil, oh-dry-one."

Frankie scraped her chair over closer to mine. "Vera, about this dry spell. Let's give you a warm up and pretend like you're meeting some chick for the first time and want to take her home or just ask her out. Do you know any good lines? Brock help her out, will ya? This may take a while."

"Ten-four, *kerrrr*. Elsie, sit down, you can play, too." He motioned them to sit. They did.

"Okay," Frankie went on, "we'll pretend like Elsie has just shown up and that I have come out of nowhere because I've seen her and we're friends." Everyone nodded their heads, good idea. Alma and Lucy eyed each other. "Now, when I sit down," Frankie said, "you think to yourself maybe I'd like to get to know this one better."

I nodded. Super, exactly what I'd been thinking since last September at Fort Apache. It couldn't have gotten any more real than this.

She went on. "Okay, now, Luce. Check my coordinates . . . good?" She motioned her arms around her chair and mine.

Lucy acknowledged them: "Good, but Vera's got to do the look-and-lean before she gets going. Alma, I'll pretend with you." She looked at Alma right in the eyes then leaned in slowly, one eyebrow arched.

"Yeah, got it, libear?" Frankie looked into me.

"Yeah," I leaned into Frankie and put both eyebrows up. I could never do the one eyebrow arch.

"Good God, Vera. You look like you're lost and need directions via a unibrow," Brock dug in.

"Shhhh, Brock, hold on. Here, let me try first . . ." Frankie leaned in to me. "So, Vera. Elsie tells me you're from Virginia. Cool state. How long have you lived there?"

"Most of my life—"

Then Alma stopped me. "Vera, you have to lean into her, too."

I did.

Frankie continued, "So what does one do in the state of Virginia for employment."

"I'm a librarian," I said.

"Now ask her a question," Brock coached.

"What do you do?" I asked my futuristic fake date.

"I'm a professional flag football player, like Elsie," Frankie stated, then slapped Elsie on the back.

"Oh, God. I can't go home with a football player. No offense, Elsie," I said.

"None taken, Veer," she squeezed her girl's hand.

Suddenly, everyone had their slant on how it should go and we were all talking and interrupting each other all at once. No one had any manners, all respect was lost. One said thus and so and the other said no, really, I have an ex-girlfriend who picked me up this way. Another said I should be more coy. One said I should be more forthcoming. I became desolate and confused. Pretty soon the conversation changed and Lucy brought us into the fact that we needed to be an entire caravan of traveling lesbians looking for a date for me. Suddenly, nobody was making sense. We were shouting and singing. Then Brock and Elsie got up and dosie doed all around our table. We were in a Virginia reel—a true state of confusion and chaos.

All the while, I discreetly scooted my chair and body closer to the dark one next to me. I was suddenly driven. Acting silly, she got us all laughing about how she nearly burned her house down when she was five because she didn't have enough paper cups full of water to put out the fire she started by igniting the fringe on her parent's bed. She said she just closed the door and hoped for the best. Every time she looked my way, I pulled my shirt down and my stomach in.

In the middle of the margarita melee and after a long while of dancing and yelling, Frankie turned to me and said, "Hey, let's continue our mock meeting. What do you say?"

I agreed.

"Sometimes," I said, "if I have a book or something in my hand, then it makes me more comfortable."

"Oh, okay. How about this?" She handed me a menu. "You can make it any book you'd like." I took it from her, and I opened it. And the play began.

"So, what are you reading there?" she asked with an eyebrow arched.

"Oh, it's just a Walt Whitman reader. Do you know him?" I arched back.

"Nope."

With my eyebrows down, I explained. "He was a great poet who lived in the nineteenth century. America's first bard of poetry. He published 'Leaves of Grass,' his magnum opus, twelve different times during his life. Poetry of the soul, poetry of the heart."

"Really? Like an amplified heart?"

I shrugged my shoulders.

Then she said, "May I see it?"

"Sure." I handed the menu to her. "You see here on page two," I pointed out, "he writes about a captain. It was the poem they found in Abe Lincoln's pocket after his assassination. 'O Captain, My Captain.' Very lyrical and beautiful."

"Really, in Lincoln's pocket? Are you a Whitman historian?" She played with me.

"No, what's your name?" I tried to play back.

"Frankie."

"No, Frankie, I'm not a Whitman historian. I'm a librarian."

"Funny, I wouldn't have pegged you as a librarian."

"Well," I said, "the clothes really intimate that I am a lumberjane of sorts and that I intend on gaining more weight, which necessitates I wear the baggy sizes."

"Lumberjane?" She laughs.

"Yeah, you know logging, cutting, hewing—that kind of thing." I felt more confident with our words.

"Do you like music, librarian?"

"Why, yes I do."

"I love music, too. Especially music you can dance to."

"Well," I tried to arch my eyebrows again, "I'm not much at dancing, Frankie."

"Who cares. You just have to feel it, right here." She grabbed my hand with her strong, veiny warm one and put it right on her stomach. Fainting, I thought, was not an option. "In the middle, you know feeling the beat, the rhythm, it's right here in the middle, like breathing in air slow and soft or fast and hard. Know what I mean?"

"Are you a music connoisseur?" I asked.

"No, a life connoisseur," she replied and smiled.

"Funny, someone told me you were a teacher."

She cocked one eyebrow at me. "You've been inquiring?" Her hand was still on mine.

I nodded.

"I think I need to leave," I said, "I'm about ready to fly this hot-dyke stand anyway."

"Hot dyke stand?" she asked.

"Yeah, you know—flannel, lipstick, mullets, trucks, that kind of thing." She rolled her head back and laughed.

"Well, librarian. Maybe I'll see you around sometime?"

"Sure. I hope so . . ."

The play ended.

"See. You've got it, Vera Curran!" She high-fived me. "You had me with you, right with you. You just need to get the number or e-mail address at the end. Got it?"

"Got it."

She grabbed my hand one more time and squeezed it. I was paralyzed.

Later that night, I thought about Walt Whitman and a poem I might write for the French thief I was in love with. Lying in my small bed in my small bungalow, I imagined lines I might recite to her if given the chance. The day on Duvall had come to a close, and I went back to all that I had seen along side of Bourdon and my friends. I thought this while my eyes were shut tight, sealed like an envelope because I wanted no one to see what the truth was that now invaded the essence of me, Vera Curran:

And, as in a waking dream I see mon frere, mon soeur,
mon amie and mon amour, ah, mon amie and mon amour -
Listen, Mon Enfants: the children of Always and of this March air,
We walk and talk and take a list onto the Open Road:

In this waking dream, a dock by a shelled sound lies
Still with seagulls fluttering about a wake, about boats -
And ferries and small skiffs motoring and tooting horns,
their bellies full of fish in the brackish water,

And weathered men full of beer at day's end,
even now in a posture of solitude, a day done,

They stand at reverent attention to a red sun just now beginning
To bear down on a horizon too soon, too brief, alas! too eternal.

As the free sun circles into her final orb, conjoined with earth
in their eternal metaphor, a reverb, brings me cataleptic
to an orange glimmer at
the water's edge, where
Some spirited girl cups my hand like a Grail, like a chalice
for my lips—
and I tell her she is red and dark and
secret.

I know, mon amour, that this day, this week, this month, this year will be a point:
still,
and eternal,
and a story for your every child - at some campfire when you're eighty - maybe
and thinking of a Tree in Louisiana - the many leaves for the healing of your nation.

Forgive me, because I
Stop. This half-hazard list is too surreal, too spatial. It is not linear.
Nor are my thoughts of you.

I am back to the sun on the list of the Open Road. I am a passing train.
What are you
doing hopping on my train?
Are you a part of July and letting freedom ring?

Are you some girl I passed on the stairs two thousand
years ago?

My have you grown.

Stop. Mon Frere. Mon Soeur. Mon Enfant. Mon Amor. Stop, please.

This is just to say that no one will ever quite tell you the way this
old school teacher can tell you -
secrets, my secrets, your secrets, our secrets:

Here, then,

I hope I can bloom into you the way you have bloomed into me.
For my labor is not
brief, nor my words, nor my heart.
For I know where seeds are planted and I know
where seeds must grow.
I know where seeds are planted;
We know where seeds must grow.

Back to the Open Road.
I am free—like the number four in our July.
Mon amour is free. Mon Amor is free.

And it will always be red and dark and secret . . .

Listen, Mon Enfants: the children of Always and of this March air!

Ringing suddenly was the phone. I orbited from my own incandescent poetry and grab for the air, for the phone.

"Yes, hello," I turned on a light.

"VERA!?"

"Yes," I rubbed the alcohol from my eyes.

"It's Frankie," she was loud and drunk. "Where did you go?"

"Oh, hey, Frank, I was just thinking about you. Where are you from?"

"I'm from Paris, France. Bite my ass. What are you doing back in your room? We've signed up Brock and Lucy to do a drag show contest. They're on in thirty minutes. Get your ass down here, libear. We're at the corner of Duvall and Third Avenue. It's called Schnicker Schnacks."

"Schnicker Schnacks. It sounds like a cracker," I said.

"If you come, I promise to dance with you."

"Then I'm staying here for sure."

"Chicken. All you have to do is sway back and forth and hold on to me. You don't even have to move your feet," she said emphatically.

"I don't know, Frankie. I was just in the middle of a good dream."

"I'm coming to get you—" *Click.*

The real show, the real plan, was about to take place, but, I did not know.

We never made it to watch the drag show where later I heard Lucy and Brock won for doing k.d. lang's "Constant Craving." Lucy was Constance and Brock was Barbra Streisand. With props from the show, they managed to pull it off. Lucy sang the song while Brock puckered his lips and echoed backup on the melody. At the end, they French kissed. It cemented the win—Barbra and k.d. in full embrace. Alma got drunk on Key Lime Margaritas and threw up three times while Barbra and Constance held her up all the way back to her room.

Instead, Frankie retrieved me from my hotel room and we walked and talked for two twilight hours into the historic district of town. Spanish moss and palm trees nestled their branches just under the luminous stars. She told me more of growing up with her mother and the hardness of the household. Evidently, she had been saved by a kind and caring grandmother who taught her to always love and fight for everything you believe in. This was part of her steadfastness, I thought. She loved everything, living mostly in the moment. She loved to sing and drink and dance and smoke, and I told her that if she had asked me first then I would have told her I already knew all of that, silly.

She loved to look up at the stars and show me which constellations she knew. Cassiopeia, the Big and Little Dippers, Orion and his belt. Gymnasium ad nauseum was her thing she said, but the constellations were a fave, too.

"Speaking of dippers"—she stopped in front of the Catholic cemetery—"we need to dip."

I stopped in my tracks. "Bourdon, we are not dipping in front of the graveyard in the middle of the night. Someone might see us."

"What? Come on you ol' asshole, a ghost? You think a ghost will see us?"

"Jesus!"

"I don't think he will either."

I stared at her with my unibrow up. "I'm afraid. Mostly embarrassed."

She cocked one eyebrow at me, then said, "What are you afraid of. I've been telling you for weeks that I would show you how to dance, you ol' asshole."

"I'm not an asshole, Bourdon. Stop calling me that!"

"Are, too. Fraidy chicken like a seventh grade girly girl."

I walked ahead of her, but she grabbed my hand and whirled me around. The top of my mongoloid head was almost face-to-face with her nose. I was looking at her neck. She reached for my other hand. I protested again.

"Shut up. Listen."

"What?" I asked.

"Do you hear the music coming from the balcony over there?"

I listened. Yes, I nodded.

"Perfect. Okay, now listen to the music and just put your arms around my waist like this." She cradled my arms around her thirty-inch frame. "Okay, now move your feet a little closer. Closer, libear. You can't be on another continent, Jesus. What's wrong with you?" I complied and moved in closer.

"Now, follow my movements—"

I interrupted. "Don't move too fast, I am as coordinated as a—"

"Shut up and just listen," she laughed.

We swayed.

"Now, how does that feel?"

"Okay."

"Bend your knees a little, libear. And, stop looking at your feet. Look at me or up to the sky or something." I did. "Okay, that's better. Now just feel the music, here." She placed her hand on my stomach. Then she slid my hand and put it on hers. I could barely look at her but did. "You know," she continued, "I never thanked you for all of your help with my small Louisa County movement."

"What, the meetings at Fort Apache and the mini-lectures on the Bible?"

"Yeah, something like that. You are a sweet woman, Vera

Curran. I never knew you were so sweet. I remember first meeting you at that stupid VEA gay alliance meeting. You looked like a mannequin holding up a prop and reading about a tree or something. You looked so cute when you dropped the book and . . ."

"Farted."

"No"—she stopped me in mid sway—"you didn't!"

"Yep. Three-point-two on the Richter scale."

"I didn't know. Plus, it wasn't that. I don't know. It was the way you looked at me. Just sweet. So sweet. It's hard to describe. You're the damn English teacher. You describe it for me."

We swayed some more then, finally I spoke. "I was afraid, nervous. Lucy and Alma had told me about you. They were trying to get us to meet. All I could manage was what I usually manage—a book and a gaseous state. I don't know how to describe it either, Bourdon."

I really did not know what to say. She had hijacked my thoughts with the swaying and the arms and the hands, everything.

"That's all right, libear. Let's just float for now."

Beyond the moon, I thought I saw what Arthur Rimbaud had once talked about in his 19th century poetry. It was something about where the sun and the ocean met, the spot where one could see eternity. It was obscure and ambiguous like my feet were before me. But I was steadied by her strong arms and hands and heart. A cacophony of feelings welled up in the cells of my throat, and multiplied like the cancer was multiplying in her.

I felt safe and loved, yet I could not breathe.

Earlier that day, I remembered a hand on mine and how I'd looked out at the ocean where the Key West horizon was kissing its Key West sky. As I danced with Frankie, it was the moon behind my girl's head. Kissing would have been perfect, but a band of naysayers walked our way. Rimbaud was dead at twenty-one but had lived like this girl was living before me. She was no Rimbaud, and he certainly was no Bourdon.

"Well?" Lucy is glaring at me while Alma flicked on my TV.

"Well, what? What time is it?" I opened my eyes to the sight of Ms. Craving herself—sash still on and Alma who looked greener than Irish moss in the rain.

"We came to find you and the Frankster. Uh-huh. Where were you? You didn't show up to the show and both of you weren't back in your rooms till after two a.m.," Lucy said.

"So . . ." I rubbed my eyes, "I didn't know the CIA was on it."

"Good God, Vera! You know what Lucy's talking about," Alma jumped in bed next to me and examined my eyes.

"Well, she's pretty," I said.

"No shit, Sherlock! Where'd you park your squad car?" Lucy dispatched me with her sarcasm.

"Come on, Veer," Alma sidled closer and winked at Lucy.

"Stop, Alma. You need to brush your teeth again," I said then sat up.

"We want the skinny or the skin," Lucy grabbed a bottled water and handed it to Alma. "We need every gory detail, Veer."

I got up to go to the bathroom. "It wasn't gory. And, no skin was involved." I shut the door.

"None?" Lucy called to me.

"Nada?" Alma was fluently retarded.

"Zilch," I came out of the bathroom and flung myself on the bed. "But—"

"But what?" they said in unison and glared at me.

"We went to the cemetery and talked." There was a long pause as we all eyed each other back and forth. I smiled.

"You took her to the Key West cemetery? Vera, are you sick?" Alma said, critiquing my pick.

"Yeah, Veer. Come on. A cemetery?" Lucy swigged from a bottle of her own and adjusted her sash. Taking her lead, I pulled on my shirt.

"Not really." I felt defensive.

The evening had spread itself against the sky. Without notice, the James River and Edgar Allan Poe surfaced to the edge of my mind. A raven dark and lurid flies above my head. Closing my eyes, I felt defeated by the judge and jury: Alma, Lucy, and ultimately, me.

I wanted to go home.

I wanted Gracie by my side and a good book.

I did not want to write poetry or think about Frankie. It was all impossible. But, I was in love with impossibility and it, I imagined, with me.

Chapter 9

"Jesu Maria! Are you two still talking about what I think you are talking about?" Momma conveyed to us in her exasperation that we needed to pick another subject.

"Grandma, what's the deal?" Kyle opened another beer.

"That's the problem"—she pointed to the beer—"you two talk and drink too much."

I absorbed this into my skin. "Yeah, right, Momma, everyone's an alcoholic but you."

"I don't drink, Vera. I never have. I don't know why you started—"

"We didn't get married in a church, Kyle," I interrupted the flow of the charge. Momma stomped away.

I patted Grace on the head and then kissed her. "In November, just eight months after our first trip, we got married, or dual destinied as she called it, standing on a rock in Key West. Just the two of us, standing before God and eternity and whatever the hell else is out there."

"Cool." He sat on the stool at the bar. "Sounds like a scene out of a Hollywood movie or something."

"Yeah, well, life's no movie, that's for sure."

"It's no sitcom either," he said, laughing at himself.

"She was weak and laughing and singing some song she always sang. I can't remember the title but it doesn't matter. She grabbed my hand, and I grabbed hers and we stood on top of some stupid rock on the salty sand. I was more afraid of slipping than anything."

"Did you?"

"What?"

"Slip? Did you slip?"

"No."

"Well, then what happened?"

"We took a picture."

"That's it?"

"Yep. Frankie pretended like she was holding up the hotel in the background. I was laughing to beat the band. So was she. Coughing and laughing. Later, we cemented our coastal vows. She was such a thief you know, Kyle."

"What do you mean, Aunt Vera?"

"She stole my heart. And, then the cancer stole her."

Key West again, and I was not at all sexy.

Back in the bungalow, I met her. Nervous, very nervous.

"I brought some wine and cheese. I know you're on a strict green bean milkshake diet. But I thought you might—"

"Open it," Frankie called from her chair by the window.

"I'm not at home, Vera. You know, I grew up in a house, Vera, a house. Good Lord, look at this view."

I looked. Nervous, I fumbled with the corkscrew.

"It's beautiful," I said. I tampered with it some more. "Uh, are you any good at these, Bourdon? My blood pressure is up, and my hands are all sweaty."

"Here," she put out her hand. It was thin and taut from the drugs and the cancer and the chemo. Despite that, she exuded the strength to open it. "Why are you nervous?" She popped the cork. I took it from her and poured one for me and one for her into the paper cups.

"You make me nervous," I said flatly and handed her the wine.

"It's five o'clock. Sorry if I make you nervous, libear," she said.

I looked at my watch.

After a minute I said, "It's just that you make me feel overwhelmed sometimes. I don't know what it is. Just standing in this room with you. For God's sake, I'm not sure what we're doing here, Bourdon. I mean, you're sick. And, then we fly down here on a whim. Then we go stand on some rock, and you suddenly ask me to marry you, or dual destiny you, and you've never even kissed me. I don't know how I'm supposed to know you or me. I didn't know which wine to buy. Jesus. I was standing in the store, and so I just bought eight bottles of red wine by looking at which pictures looked the prettiest. And, forget about the cheese. I feel like I've kidnapped you. Your mother is going to kill me. And, then there's Lucy and Brock and—"

She grabbed my hand. "Shut up."

"No, I'm not going to shut up. You dragged me here on some *From Here to Eternity* final farewell trip, and I feel like a hostage. Bourdon, you can't do this to me."

"Do what, Vera? Do what? What am I doing to you?" She dropped my hand and walked back to the window.

"You can't sing and dance and play and fart and—" I stopped. "You can't die on me, Bourdon! I haven't even kissed you."

It was clear that that was the point.

Frankie was still.

I breathed in.

She got up and walked toward me.

I held my breath.

"Vera?" she asked.

"Yes."

"When's the last time you made love?"

"1863. Wild Southern belle, your age, I believe." I sipped my wine.

"Come on, libear, be serious. When is the last time you took a good roll in the hay?"

"I think it's been ten years," I said flatly. "And, that was only because I was trying to make up for a lost steak."

"A steak?" She grimaced.

"I had thrown a steak onto the lawn during a heated argument. I got so mad at her I just chucked the steak out the back door. I tried to rectify the situation by suggesting sex. Later, I retrieved the steak, brushed it off and ate. Much better than the sex."

The guffaw that came from Frankie would not stop.

"It's not that funny. Stop. What are you laughing at?"

"You, libear."

"Well, what's so funny. It was an expensive steak. I wasn't going to—"

Then, she was there in front of me as if the rug had pulled taut, magically pitting us two together. I sucked in. We said nothing. Face-to-neck, shoulder-to-head. We stood. An iridescent aroma arrived from her mouth to cup the air in front of my nose. Mixed with it was her olive Coppertone skin. I looked away, but she turned me toward her.

"What are you doing, Bourdon? You're making me nervous again."

"I'm going to kiss you. Is that okay, you ol' asshole?"

"I guess, but," I said, hesitating.

"But what?"

"I'm concerned about my nose."

"You're concerned about your nose? Your nose is fine. What's wrong with your nose?"

"Stuff in them, maybe. With buying the wine and the cheese and all, I haven't had time to check. And, then, then there's my stomach." I looked down.

"Vera Curran. Look up in the air." I obliged, but felt slightly threatened. "There isn't a damn thing growing up in there. Pull up your shirt." I hesitated. "Come on, Fifi, pull up your shirt." I must have looked incredulous. "Pull up your shirt before I do." She paused. "Vera, if you don't pull up your shirt . . ."

That was enough. I sucked in as hard as I could so that my three rolling hills would become less hill-ish and more mound-ish. I was embarrassed. By the time I did this, Frankie was on her knees face-to-face with my intestines. Running was no good. I'm stuck. Placing her hands directly on top of mine at the edge of my skirted shirt, Frankie helped me to pull and expose even more of the bleached white underside of a whale. I jerked, pulled my hands away, and my shirt was over Frankie's head. We are stuck like a cocoon.

When she kissed me there, I winced.

"VERA!"

"What?" I looked wildly about for myself.

"You're beautiful. Your skin is so soft." Wrapping her arms

around my waist, I looked to see the light glimmering through the window, pouring itself over the line of carpet that led to the now one body, shapeless, like an amoeba. The sun spired arcs and shadows across the creases of my eyes. All I could do, all I could do was place my hands on the spine of the girl who was now a prisoner under my shirt.

Caressing the overtures of my belly, Frankie kissed me. Her lips like warm petals heating my soul, my skin, my life. For what felt like forever, she stayed there with me—stayed and stayed and stayed, kissed and kissed and kissed. I was hot all over suddenly, and my knees jerked involuntarily. The swelling inside me burgeoned from the back of my neck to the inside curve of my elbows to the spaces I had forgotten existed. If Sappho were alive, I thought, she would have fainted, too.

I put my hands on her head and pushed my hands through her thick, dark hair. "I'm not sure," I dryly sputtered, "how to—"

"Vera, don't talk," Frankie said. Slowly she unveiled herself. Her hair all static and my body electric. I was stiller than still. Pulling herself up over the tightrope of my body, she came to me with her eyes. She leaned back and we became arcs, like divers, and she pulled my shirt right off of my body.

Here I was. Here I was. Vera Curran, unclothed, half-naked.

"I want you to feel my heart. Put your hand on my heart." I did. "Can you feel it beating?" I looked down at her breasts. "No, Vera. Look at me. Can you feel it beating?" She cupped her hand over mine, then put her other on my left breast. "I can feel yours. Don't stop looking at me. Can you do that, libear?"

"I haven't ever—"

When she lowered her face to mine, it was all I could do to stay standing. A light surely pierced the foggy steam my body was emitting. I knew fire. I knew the torch. I knew the song. My breath had stopped, and I could not catch the thick air into my lungs that hung between us. Precariously slow and with her eyes locked into mine, she pressed her lips into mine and the way the flower of her air bloomed like oxygen into my veins was steadily increased by the movement, the rolling, and then, finally, her tongue joined mine in an inexplicable union, and I felt newly baptized. I knew joy. I knew Frankie. I was alive. Apart, then back again. The realm of possibility completed. Apart, then back again. The ache, the pressure, the smell, the eyes. I bloomed back into her as she had bloomed into me. Running my hands up her back, I pressed her into me, she pressed into me. We squeezed the pulp from one another and our oils and sweat and lips began the bond that boiled out and into the surreal blue canvass that lovemaking does.

I had forgotten my body did this.

I was out of breath. We parted. Frankie was out of breath. I had no words. She had no words. We did it again.

The fog was thick. I had no skin. It had been stolen by a French thief. Where were my lips? Where were my eyes? I could not hear! What did I have to offer this thief?

A dance.

"You know the story about the night swan?" Frankie said. She was up beside the bed. Darkness slanted in with the bent yellow light of the fading sun. I reached to touch her shoulder. She slid her hand into mind.

"No, Bourdon. I don't. This isn't the part where you get all charming and tell me parables, and then I have to go and cry? Your pulling my shirt over my head has pretty much done me in for the night."

"The night swan swims only at night because he's afraid of the daylight. That it will show his ugliness. So, during the day, he hides in the underbrush, and at night he comes out to swim on the lake."

"How does he know he's ugly?" I asked.

"He doesn't. It's just in him."

"That's it? Does he have any friends ol' parable one?"

"Yeah. Two. A turtle and a fish."

"Are they ugly too?"

"No. They just are what they are." She paused and squeezed my hand. "Vera?"

"Yeah, night swan."

"Will you write my eulogy?"

"Who am I, Bourdon? The turtle or the fish?"

"You, libear, you are the lake."

"What do you mean?"

"Well, here it is. Before you write my eulogy, throw a rock in a lake or a river or something, and then you'll understand."

"Kiss me, you criminal," I said. She laughed and did.

We kissed all night.

Like the touch of her hands had once stayed with me for three days, the kisses would chap and burn my lips for many days and nights to come. The heat and the healing suffused into my skin, bone to muscle.

At least until Easter.

Chapter 10

I was weaker than I thought.

Five months after our second trip to Key West, Frankie was taken away in an ambulance to St. Mary's Hospital. We were together at my home in Louisa—better at my home because she was sick and couldn't manage on her own in her small apartment. Grace loved the daily company, and I raced home from work to do the things necessary for her care. Her mother refused to visit the den of iniquity.

I was awakened early to her breathless breathing and saw no other option. Scared, I dialed 911. Even though it was a week before Easter, the Virginia weather was chilly—always fickle like Eileen Bourdon.

More than a year had passed since the Louisa County School Board had driven her away, and the high school had found a remote reason to not invite Frankie back for a second year. It all seemed to come oddly to fruition. Frankie couldn't have worked in the fall anyway, so she spent hours writing to congressmen and doing bits with the VEA alliance she was so loyal to.

I hadn't seen Eileen Bourdon in months, but now we were together again—Eileen and me and her daughter. I had called her on the way to the hospital as a courtesy. This time, however, the tone was much different from any familial coffee I had ever shared with her.

When we got a room for Frankie, this was when the troubles really began. I was unaware that her mother would be as hostile as she turned out to be, like a switch had rewired itself in the months that her daughter and I had been together.

The conflagration began with the worst of euphemisms:

"You self-centered dyke bitch. Do you really think I'd let you in here? Do you have any idea what you have done to my daughter? She's tired. She's been tired since you took her to Key West and stayed a week. You have no right coming in here." Eileen said this while she stood with an orchid in her hand in front of room 514 in ICU.

"Why are you doing this? Why are you so mad at me? At Frankie?" It was the least I could say but also the most.

"She's my daughter—" She then changed the subject. "Have you not heard of House Resolution Bill seven-fifty-one my dear?"

"No," I hadn't. I really hadn't. Frankie might.

"Well, it's no resolution anymore. It has been law since last July, and it states emphatically that only family can be allowed to visit a family member in the hospital. Got it?"

From behind the nurse's station, a few nurses looked our way. My cover was blown—they know I'm on the rainbow committee. I wished for Brock to be here. He would know what to do. I was desperate to see my girl.

"Eileen, all I want to do is see her. I know she's dying but can't you find it within yourself . . ."

Just then, Alma and Lucy walked in. Thank God. Brock must have called them after I called him. They both sidled up to me. Lucy put her hands on her hips.

"Don't even try to come and see her or any of your dyke friends," she looked at them. "I will have you arrested." Her face was red. "Do you understand?"

Lucy grabbed my shirt. "Come on, Veer. Let's go before she turns us in as Sodomites and then we have to arrest the whole state of Virginia."

I stopped her and mustered up a cup of courage. I looked at Eileen Bourdon and said, "How did you have her then?"

"What did you say?" She brandished me a scowl.

"How did you have her then? How were you gifted with such a beautiful daughter. It must have been an act of love and mercy on God's part for you. I don't understand how you can go on breathing the same breath I breathe, that Frankie breathes, that we all breathe." I trembled. Alma pulled on my shoulder, but I was firm and distant from everyone as if I was in a tunnel. "Why and how? How is it possible? Can you tell me?"

"You don't know what it means to be a mother. You are so sinful that even God made that a problem for you and your likes. I hope you burn in hell with your baggy clothes and manly hair and fat body. You are disgusting. You even smell like a homosexual. Get out of my face before I slap you into the next century. Get away from me, my daughter and my family. You can't possibly know what a family is. You have nothing to compare it to." Eileen turned on her heels and closed the door behind her as she entered Frankie's room.

I tried to see in but to no avail.

"Why Lucy?" I asked then put my head on her shoulder.

"It's not ours to figure out, Vera. We just need to do what

we've always done in a situation like this," Lucy looked at Alma, then to me.

"What are you talking about, Lucy?" Alma looked worried.

"You know the Lord's Prayer, don't you, Alma?"

"Of course."

"Well, I know Vera knows the words. I've got the millennium's newest way to crash a party."

"What are you talking about, Lucy?" Alma said as we moved to the elevators.

"Well, if it's going to work, we're going to need a lot of praying and a lot of makeup. And, Alma, don't call me Lucy, honey. You know the name is Constance. Constance Craving," she winked at us. "Alma, turn on your cell. We need to call Barbra."

And, with that, we walked out of the hospital and went directly to Freddy's to create the master plan.

"So, you guys made up a plan to crash Frankie's hospital room?" Kyle put his feet up on the coffee table while Momma dusted around the furniture.

"Yep, we sure did."

"Vera, can you just stop talking about it. Please?" Momma held the can of Pledge and faced Kyle and me.

"Why, Grandma?"

"Because in all of this you have to remember that Eileen Bourdon lost her daughter. It's not just about you and what happened to you. A mother lost her daughter. Not only did she lose her once, but she lost her twice—"

"Twice?" I asked.

"Yes. And, Kyle you may not want to hear this and Vera maybe you either. But parents lose their children to your lifestyle. You may not want to hear it, but it's the darn truth," she paused. "Kyle, lift your feet," she resumed her dusting. "Why don't you all talk about that for a change instead of yourselves. Mommas who have gay kids struggle with their feelings, too. We want the best, and, dammit, I have to agree with Eileen. This is not the best lifestyle for our children."

"What is, Grandma? A dad who never pays attention to you. A dad who plays golf every weekend with his buddies and stays drunk every Friday, Saturday and Sunday of your entire life. But, hey, it's okay because he's straight and has a good lookin' wife who's on the PTA and turns her head when he goes on business trips and sleeps with the wives of the husbands he plays golf with? Is that lifestyle better?"

"I'm leaving." She put the can of Pledge down. "You two wouldn't understand a thing I have to say."

"Mom, don't go," I got up and put my hand on her. "Kyle and I don't want you to go. I understand what you're saying. Right, Kyle?" I glanced at him, then glared.

"Yeah, right," he managed.

"We all lost her, Mom. You have a good point."

"Well, I thought so, too." She sat down on the couch.

"Aunt Vera. How does she have any point?" Kyle got up.

"Stop, Kyle," I put my hand up. He sat back down.

"All of us, including me, have to understand this. Momma, you are exactly right. Parents of gay children lose their hope of the normal life for their children. Or, at least what they perceive as a normal life for their children. And, Momma, correct me if I'm wrong. Parents are ashamed to admit they are ashamed. It tarnishes them, too. They do lose a child to homosexuality. But, Momma, you need to understand that we children lose our parents through our own shame. We run away because we have disappointed the hell out of you. We are perfect up until it all comes out, and then it's a godforsaken mess. With all puns intended. We're sorry, Momma. We're sorry. We're sorry." I broke down and cried.

"Well, I didn't want you to go and cry, Vera. Jesus."

"Yeah, Aunt Veer. Don't cry." Kyle gave me a tissue.

My eyes burned. "Well, I can't help it. But I do have one thing to say, Alma and Lucy and Brock are the best friends ever. I couldn't have made it to this point without them"—I stopped and wiped my face—"and, you too, Momma."

She got up and went for the kitchen and said nothing.

"Tell me about the plan, Aunt Vera. Talk it out. Maybe it will help."

I'd always wanted to be Captain Kirk.

"Ten-four. *Kerrr,*" Lucy hung up her cell phone. "Brock will be here in fifteen. Alma, take notes. Vera, let's talk dyke."

"What?" I asked.

"Listen, Eileen Bourdon is never letting you near your girl again, so we have to hash out a plan to get you in the hospital. She's probably going to have a vigil day and night with Christian Go-A-Licktion, so we need to get by them using their own tactics."

"Go-A-Licktion." Alma was spelling.

"Anything's better than *coalition.*" Lucy winked. I laughed and smacked her on the back of the head.

Elsie came with the drinks. "Sorry to hear about Frank, Vera! Anything I can do?"

Lucy sipped her margarita. "As a matter of fact, Elsie. We may be able to fit you in the plan. Be ready for some linebacking!"

"Hey, you can count on me for any of that. If you need any other 'backers, let me know."

"Roger that!" Alma kept writing.

Within fifteen minutes, Lucy had explained how we were all going to get on the fifth floor of St. Mary's and get to see Frankie. Luckily, Luce was the director for the League of Nurses and Brock actually worked there. We all had an in except Alma and me which was okay because Brock had a "friend" who made ID badges for the staff. The problem was getting me in because I was so recognizable.

Brock overheard the last part as he swaggered in. "Don't worry about that, Vera. Or, should I say, Vinny? Vinny. Your new name. We can't dress you like a drag queen to get you in the hospital, Vera. We got to dress you up like a king."

"Oh, no. What exactly are you guys up to?"

"Vera, remember. I tried to put makeup on you one time? You see where that got you." Lucy winked at Brock.

"Remember, Vera: Vinni, Vidi, Bici: Vinny came, she saw, she got bitchy. Girl, you're gonna show those nurses at St. Mary's just what you're made of. And Bitchy Bourdon ain't gonna know what hit her."

It took nearly twenty-four hours to hash out the plan. Brock got the IDs and Lucy bought hair products and formulas and all of the accoutrements to make it a go. Alma directed and I followed like a lost puppy in a rainstorm. We drank beer and smoked and high-fived till there wasn't much more to high-five about. We had to get going. I wanted to see Frankie more than anything. I burned with apprehension. My breath was in my lungs yet I could not exhale. I read, weirdly, from Psalms to comfort my personal transgressions and every now and then rethought my own sexuality. Was I going to be marred by this shame all of my life. How would I? How could I get through the stigma which was branded into my DNA as strongly as the propensity I had for the women I loved—emotionally and physically.

When we showed up at the hospital, my band of travelers and I looked as ready for a room-busting as any travelers could get. The law of the Virginia land was going to be usurped by the band of criminals who arrived at the steps of the escalator to begin the journey to room 514.

It was Easter Sunday and I hadn't seen Frankie in several days. I had thought of all of the things I would say once in the room with her, but once in the elevator, Lucy and Brock got the giggles and then everything drained from my brain. Alma looked official in her white coat and hospital badge. Lucy had on her nursing director's outfit and Brock held my hand. I was my childhood star, Captain Kirk, in a gold shirt and dark pants—but perhaps these days better matched to a shorter version of James Brolin who was actually married to Barbra Streisand, a.k.a., in this case, Brock Goldberg.

I had never in my life had so much hairspray in my hair. The padding around my shoulders and arms and legs made me hot and itchy. And the sweat across my temple began to commingle with the gray hair spray used to fake the salt-and-pepper look. We were good imitations to the unsuspecting eye—just an old married couple in from New York wanting to see their niece before she died. To Eileen Bourdon, lung specialists in from Dartmouth to see if there is another course of treatment. All, of course, had been okayed through the hospital's director of oncology: Constance Carver. Alma was her traveling intern.

Luckily, Bourdon was nowhere to be seen once we got on the fifth floor. A couple of unknowns were hanging around the nurse's station, but people barely acknowledged we were all in drag. I couldn't believe it. We were making it down the hallway. Just as we got to the room, a nurse stopped us for a second to ask. Barbra took her hand and said something about how when God shuts one door he opens another and how awfully worried about her niece she's been. Without hesitation, she showed us all to the door. One at a time was her only counsel. I broke through the door. My heart thumped like a wild beast.

"Hey there. Can I help you?" the strained voice came. Oxygen lifted itself in a cage off to itself while a monitor flashed red numbers and rhythmic beats. A white orchid sat on the table beside her.

"It's me!"

"Who?" An eyelid opened.

"Vera." I walked closer.

"Have I died?"

"No, you ol' asshole. It's really me!"

"Libear." She exhaled and moved her thin hand toward me.

"Yeah, libear. It's me," I was beside her with my hand near hers.

"You look funny!" Her voice was weak, and she put her hand over mine. We clenched our hands together. I sat down next to her.

"Well, I told Brock I wanted to be a lumberjane, but he told me that he wouldn't have any of that if I was going to be his wife."

"Wife. I thought you were my wife, but now that I see you . . . My, what big arms we have, my dear!" She squeezed the padding of my shoulder.

"And what big eyes you have, my dear," I looked at her.

"And what a big mouth you have my dear." She laughed, and so did I.

"Kiss me, you criminal," she said.

I leaned down and kissed her cool dry lips. That familiar feeling overcame me—a flood of nerves and cells commingled with the love I felt for her when so close.

"Will you still be my wife even if you've changed sexes?" she whispered.

"Of course I will. It makes it more legal this way, eh?"

"As long as you stay the same libear, I don't care what sex you are," she said as she closed her eyes. Then after a moment, she said, "Hey, you know, I'm sorry about the children."

She wasn't making sense. "What do you mean, children?" I asked.

"At Louisa."

"You've lost me Frankie."

"Well, as usual, you're not listening. Do I have to yell?"

"I'm sorry about them, too," I said in conciliation. "Tired?"

"Yeah. A little. How's the gang? Lucy, Alma, Brock?"

"They're outside keeping a vigil. If Lucy and Brock break out into song, then we'll have to kidnap you and take you out of here."

"Like in Key West when I kidnapped you?"

"You didn't kidnap me in Key West, Bourdon. I went willingly on the plane with you."

"No, not that time, Vera." She was suddenly serious. "The time when we all went. Remember when I called you while they were doing Constance and Barbra, and we went to the cemetery, and I taught you how to dance. Remember?" I nodded. "You kept looking at your stupid feet, and we only swayed because I was too afraid to teach you how to tango."

"Tango. You never even said anything about tango that night," I admonished her slightly.

"Funny, I knew you were scared. From the second I met you, and you dropped the poem about the stupid tree in Louisiana to the Post-its to the smokes at Apache. You were always nervous around me. Weren't you?"

"The tree in Louisiana is not stupid, Bourdon," I said emphatically. She breathed heavy.

"Tell me about it, then," she said and closed her eyes.

From memory, I recited the lines by Walt Whitman:

I saw in Louisiana a live-oak growing,
All alone stood it and the moss hung down from the branches,
Without any companion it grew there uttering joyous leaves of dark green,
And its look, rude, unbending, lusty, made me think of myself,
But I wonder'd how it could utter joyous leaves standing alone there without its friend near, for I knew I could not,
And I broke off a twig with a certain number of leaves upon it, and twined around it a little moss,
And brought it away, and I have placed it in sight in my room,
It is not needed to remind me as of my own dear friends,
(For I believe lately I think of little else than of them,)
Yet it remains to me a curious token, it makes me think of manly love;
For all that, and though the live-oak glistens there in Louisiana solitary in a wide flat space,
Uttering joyous leaves all its life without a friend a lover near,
I know very well I could not.

Without warning, I burst into tears. In spasms, my stomach blew in and out and hesitated at each guttural sob. I tried my best to mute each by holding my breath. But, they came anyway. Frankie smiled at me from the bed and held my hand, and we did not speak for a long while. Finally, she did.

"Yep, it was some tree. Why does he take from the tree do you think?"

"I think he wants a remembrance of it and why it's doing what it's doing," I wiped the tears away with my bare hand. "But I don't know."

"Don't fret over this and me, you know. I won't have any of

it, Vera. You understand? Everything has been good. My life has been good. You have been good—"

"But, I don't want to be a tree!"

"Vera, you're not going to be a tree, dammit. You can move your legs. Quit standing still in your stupid library and live a little will ya? Listen, libear, look in the side drawer near your bed when you get home. I've left you a Post-it note."

We paused again. I nodded that I would and said to her that I would try and live a little. I bent down from my own undergrowth and lay my head next to hers. We remained, unspeaking for what seemed like many minutes, till a knock came at the door. It was the nurse—time for more treatments. From behind her stood the three amigos. Frankie looked at them and smiled. She whispered in my ear, and I whispered back. I kissed her hands and then she kissed mine.

And, then I left. I didn't look back.

It was the last time I saw her alive.

Chapter 11

The spider sprouted legs in my brain.

Easter weekend was upon us while the walls of deception grew hairy and stilted in my heart. I walked ahead of Brock and Alma and Lucy. Ironically, my thoughts came to a quote that I blurted out to Brock:

"What a tangled web we weave, when we first practice to deceive." I smiled back at him.

"What are you talking about, Veer?" He began to wipe off some of his makeup.

"I don't know." But when I saw Eileen Bourdon emerge from her white suburban, I did.

Brock saw it, too. "Let's say we make like a bakery truck and haul buns this way," he pointed. Moving from him, I crouched slightly.

No way, I thought. I felt the creep within me.

Once in front of me, she stopped and put her hands on her hips as if to say, well, well, what have we got here.

Brock wiped the lipstick across his face as if the Indian in him was coming out. Behind me, Alma and Lucy stood frozen. We waited.

Eileen leaned to one side, then finally spoke, "Well—" And that was all I allowed.

"Hey, Eileen." My fangs squirted the spit. "Got Jesus or just a dying dyke? Which is it that you really have?"

Then we pounced.

Brock and Alma and Lucy surrounded us. Tufts of Eileen's hair stuck to my leggy body and then flew into orbit, landing on the sidewalk. I was stuck so hard to her I thought I would pass through her to the other side, a metaphoric irony that I did not want to play out. Lucy screamed at me, but I didn't hear her. After thirty seconds of incisive barbs, I wanted release. She was the female spider, and I the male. She was defeating me, pushing me down. I felt my abdomen crushing down, an arachnid under a religious shoe. Then, out of nowhere, I bit—on what I did not know till her eight-legged grip released me from sure death. It was her nipple, and it came clean off. Screaming all the way to her car, Eileen held her right breast while I lay around the web of my friends, waiting for my tarantula to die. I had bitten the spider.

I yelled, "Just pretend you're an Amazon, Eileen! They didn't need their right tits anyway. Next time, just shoot me with a bow and arrow."

"Come on, Captain Kirk, or whoever you are!" Brock lifted me. "We need to get you out of here before the police show up and our best laid schemes of drag queens and men go astray."

Alma helped me brush off my suit, "Roger that. Good grief, Veer, I thought you were going to kill her!"

"Yeah, Vera," Lucy exhorted, "you certainly did get *bici*!"

"Veni, vidi!" Brock laughed.

"Holy Cow, Aunt Vera!" Kyle screamed and then jumped ten feet in the air, "I can't believe it. You kicked her ass!"

"Yeah, I guess you could say that! Come here, Grace." Gracie-Mac sidled up.

"What happened then? Did you see her again?"

"Frankie?"

"No, Eileen?"

"No, not until the funeral. It was the last time I saw her."

Kyle brought himself down, "Oh, God, I'm so sorry, Aunt Vera!"

He hugged me. "Want a beer?"

"Not now. Maybe later."

"Don't tell me Granny is influencing you? Because if she is—"

I interrupted. "No, the only influence on me was that damn girl. That Bourdon sure did screw me up."

"Screw you up? How?" he asked.

"Well, if I hadn't fallen for her, I never would have gotten married or dual destinied, and I never would have gotten in the religious issue with the right wing, nor would I have changed my voting status from Republican to Democrat. Nor would I have been arrested and had a restraining order placed on me by Eileen and her family—" I stopped the train.

"She died that Easter, Kyle. But it was I who rose up."

"Hurry up," he interrupted, "Granny is driving up from the store."

• • •

At Hollywood cemetery on a cool Wednesday in April, Frankie Bourdon, the ex-Navy pilot turned gym teacher, did not get a twenty-one gun salute. The Bourdons did not pull it together for her. They were more worried about having police presence in case I came back for the second nipple. But, just beyond the small hill where they carried her body, I found a spot behind President John Tyler where no one could see me. The James River was below me where the Class V Hollywood rapids flustered themselves high and mighty over the rocks that bore out their hydraulics—back and forth, the rush resounded. It interfaced my heart. I had not said good-bye to her.

Grace and her rainbow collar (now donned with a Key West insignia) stayed in the shadow behind me. I closed my eyes and tried to remember her hands the last time she touched me. The vision did not come. I was by myself. I was not with her. I was Spanish moss hanging on to a dead President. The chatter of her voice rang in and out of my brain: "Hey, you asshole. Come here and kiss me! . . . Libear, dance with me! . . . Quit looking at your feet! . . . Jesus, it's not a date or anything! . . . Just beer and cigarettes galore about our very important lives at Freddy's cafe! . . . I'm coming to get you . . . Libear, can you teach me . . ." And with the last one, I cried. The rivulets coursed down my cheeks onto Grace's head.

For an entire month after Frankie's death, I listened to her "Amplified Heart" CD, driving up and down Interstate 250. I quit my job after Holt Meyers, his girlfriend and Marty Hanna and his band of choristers had sent me a condolence note about how I had lost such a good friend. Frankie was no friend to me. I handed in my resignation to the principal who barely knew I had been there for twenty years. After taking out some money for retirement, I decided to take time off and do whatever it was that I was supposed to do. Driving up and down the highway listening to Frankie's music was the best I could do.

On the last day of April, nearly a month after the funeral, Grace and I sat alone on my deck. With a cold beer in between my legs, I lit the chimenea then looked at the night stars. Like Holden Caulfield felt alone at seventeen, I was alone, too. I wanted his hunting cap on backward and a cold trip to New York City to find where the ducks took his pond. Suddenly, I recalled what Frankie had once told me to do—throw a rock into a lake and watch or something like that. I didn't know, I couldn't remember. Alma and Lucy had tried to get me to go to the March on Washington where everyone would be. I said no thanks. Even ol' Elsie had stopped by with her band of flag footballers to see if I wanted to catch a ride with them. I said no, no, no. I didn't want to go.

Three beers into my meditation on the fire, the phone rang. I didn't answer it. Fifteen minutes later, it rang again. It was Alma and Lucy for sure. I leaned into the fire and added pine needles, pine cones and dried up sticks from my backyard. My two big pines are sheltered by the night sky.

T.S. Eliot was right, April was the cruelest of months. Goddamned defector. My thoughts were random, and the phone rang again. Grace stole more pats from me as I ignored it again. It was then that I noticed my hands. I had never spent much time inspecting my hands. My nails were short, the lines neat and even, the fingers spread out even and nicely. Then I saw hers—Frankie's hands—on top of mine, a specter sudden, unexpected. A dense firelight built up. Two pine cones lit up with dancing flames. High bit-rate ballerinas doing the funky chicken and swirling their orange and yellow orbs quickly, then ever-so-slowly. The flaming pine cones were cheek to cheek, an odd dueling fireball. I looked around to see if anyone was near. The rush of the wind had jolted me slightly. My eyes fell back on the two flames.

And, then, it hit me. It hit me like I had been in a closed chrysalis state my whole life. Nearly falling out of my chair, I looked up to the sky, then back down wildly at the flames. I checked the sky once more. For five more minutes, I continued this weird ritual. Finally, one of the dancing flames grew smaller and smaller while the other remained strong and proud. Pretty soon, the smaller flame conjoined like the best of metaphors into the bigger one. The small flame was no more, but the larger flame remained.

The phone rang.

I jumped to my feet, my hair sticking straight up from my own electricity. I wanted to scream but was too scared. Running like a banshee, I went into the house and clamored for the phone.

"Hello?" I exhaled.

"Goddamn it, Vera. What in the hell are you doing. I've been ringing your horn for nearly two hours. Are you okay?" It was Brock with some musical booming in the background.

"Oh, hey, Brock. I'm glad you called. I need to ask you something. You're good at quotes, right?"

"Vera, I'm in a mood. No quotes tonight. I'm hungry. Have you had dinner?"

I pressed on. "Brock, listen. What is the bird that comes out of the ashes? I can't remember. My mind is drawing a blank. Do you know?"

"Honey, a bird that comes out of asses?" Brock was a goddamned comic, I thought.

"Brock, I'm not kidding around. What's the name of the bird?"

There was a pause, then, "Uh, let's see. A bird that comes out of the ashes. I think it's a fated kind of a reference. Vera, have you been drinking?"

"Is it a nightingale, Brock? For God's sake, think. It starts with an f, I believe."

"Look, Veer, the only word that I like that starts with an f is . . ."

"Brock, shut up! I'm hanging up."

He yelled from the other end, "No, Vera! Don't hang up. Give me a second. Hmm. Finch. No. Firebird. No, that's a bad car. No. Oh, I got it, you dork. It doesn't start with a f, Vera. It starts with a p. It's a phoenix. The phoenix rises from the asses," he laughed.

I laughed, then said, "Brock. I need to tell you a secret."

"You have been drinking. Good girl. What's up. Tell Uncle Brocky."

"Can you pick me up in the morning and take me to D.C.?"

"Why?"

"Well, part of it is that I want to hook up with Alma and Lucy. The other part, I'll tell you on the ride."

"Having a change of heart are we about going to the Millennium March?"

"Not really. But there is one thing I have to do. It will set me straight with Frankie."

"Veer." Brock stopped me. "You were gay with Frankie."

"Brock, I'm really hanging up this time!"

"Stop. I'm sorry. What time?"

"Seven thirty sharp. And, don't be late."

"Seven thirty! Jesus, Vera! I'm going to have to stay up all night."

"Can you?" I pleaded.

"I'll bring the lattes from Freddy's, no problem."

"Brock?"

"Yeah?"

"I love you."

And like Frankie, he said, "I love your ass, too!"

I sat up all night to prepare Frankie's eulogy.

On the way to Washington, Brock told me that Oprah said that everything happened for a reason. I told Brock to tell Oprah I didn't care about fate or destiny or any of that New Age stuff. Believing in that stuff made my stomach turn. Crystals and candles and lotions that touted therapies for everything. Not me. Nope.

Via cellular, we connected with Alma and Lucy on the Washington Mall. My plan was to do what Frankie had wanted to do eighteen months earlier. Take her small Louisa movement and shout it to the world at the Millenium March. Bourdon couldn't make it to the scene of the crime, so I was her substitute.

Lucy found the roster of speakers and asked a friend of hers and Frankie's from Human Rights Campaign if I could be squeezed in to say a few words on Frankie's behalf. No one knew if it was possible. But looking at the line of marchers with their rainbow hats and stickers and the drag queens and the police not protecting them but the enclave of Mathew Sheppard haters, I thought any damn thing was possible. Here I was. A conservative librarian from Louisa, Virginia, trying to get on stage with Anne Heche and Ellen DeGeneres. Hilarious.

After two hours of parking, walking, calling, finding, getting lost and doing street diversions, we made it to the sound staging area. Large luminous television sets and speakers stood like Gulliver in the middle of Lilliput.

Brock gave me a rainbow hat that I immediately turned around backward. Alma held Gracie-Mac while we tried to find our HRC buddy to get in place to speak. There were a million fags and dykes marching and the confusion was like trying to get a drink at Freddy's on margarita night. Everyone was dancing and yelling and wreaking havoc. Some people were paying attention to some football player discussing his coming out story.

Suddenly, Lucy grabbed my arm. "Vera, you're up. I think we can get you up there!"

I hesitated then reached into my pocket. I pulled out a Post-it from Frankie. *What do women do? Women fly* is all it said. It was the last one she'd given me. I had never written her back.

Out of the corner of my eye, I saw Ellen and Anne as I tried to reach the podium. Suddenly, Ellen broke out in a dance that made the crowd roar. Music was playing and our fag football star was done. The mall was up and dancing to Ellen on the big screen. Vera Curran was told to wait. I looked down at the note again, and before I knew it, an HRC rep was asking me to get off of the stage. Ellen was up. And, who could usurp her?

My plan was to talk about Frankie, to talk about how she'd come to Louisa County and why she wanted to see her small movement of teaching homosexuality in the classroom get started and why it was important and what the Bible really said and how could those four main points in it have screwed us all up for two thousand years. I'd written the epistle of all epistles that established all of her main points, and now I was told that the podium was not mine.

Frankie was dead. Her movement dead. I was left standing with a Post-it note in my hand and no voice in front of a quarter of a million people. No one could see me. No one could hear me. My voice had been mute for a thousand years. My master plan had failed.

I was helped off the podium by my friends, Lucy, Alma and Brock. We drove away from there to spend an early evening in Richmond drinking margaritas with Elsie.

Kyle stopped me in the middle of the Millennium's biggest non-speech. Momma told me to stop and to get Grace off of her lap.

Then Kyle asked if we could do what I'd been wanting to do all weekend. Go see Frankie. We agreed. Kyle turned off his recorder, psychology 201 and the root causes of whatever. Enough said, and Kyle insisted that he would write a paper about homophobia, Aunt-Vera style for his professor.

I said okay.

Chapter 12

Rites of passage have their costs, but I was stronger than I thought.

When I was nearly forty years old, I had a relationship with a girl named Frankie Bourdon. I didn't think she stood any chance of ever getting anything done in Louisa County, and I wasn't sure if she'd even ever considered liking me. But, in the end, she did both, much to my doubting chagrin.

I remember as a little girl standing on the edge of the Grand Canyon and eternity. Among the purple and yellow wildflowers, a small voice inside of me spoke—a small ripple, a rock perhaps in the lake. I had told myself, as I recalled, like good librarians should, that to always remember that day, that I would come back later in life to remember how I felt. Remember the wind in my hair, my small hands, my small feet, my mismatched outfit and my strange family on the other side of the road. It was my strange home calling me, telling me there were great things inside, things I didn't understand yet at seven, but would later. My strange homes were everywhere: with Holden Caulfield and Captain Kirk; with Arthur Rimbaud and T.S. Eliot, Walt Whitman; with Matthew, with Mark, and Luke and John; with Sodom and Gomorrah; with Leviticus, with Paul, with Jesus, with Brock, Lucy and Alma; with Peter Van Hedron and his spidery gang; with Holt Meyers and his lisp; with Maggie Winterfield and her father; with Eileen Bourdon, her Old and New Testaments aligned. Yes, even with her. Memories and still points everywhere. But the briefest still moment of my life is the eighteen months I spent with that crazy gym teacher, Frankie. She was my truth and I, I suppose, was hers.

Bourdon gave me three things: an arsenal of yellow Post-it notes, a rainbow collar for my dog and, for the first time in nearly forty years, my life.

She, in retrospect, was my Revelation 22. Her leaves were for the healing of my own personal nation. And that was the root cause of that.

Now, as Kyle and Momma and Gracie and I visited her grave in Hollywood Cemetery, I see her strong hands interfaced with mine.

Over her grave, Kyle managed to say that she was the best. It was the least he could say, but the most also.

"Move over, Grace. Big ball of yellow slobber, I can't see," Momma nudged Gracie over. While next to Frankie's headstone, I dug a small hole in the ground (with Gracie's help) underneath an orchid Eileen Bourdon had put there. Out of my pocket I pulled out a Post-it note. An answer to hers, finally. I showed what I wrote to Momma and Kyle and then kissed it. I carefully placed it in the dirt and covered it up, then gently returned the orchid.

Later, I would call my friends and take them and Kyle and Momma to Freddy's to talk about our very important lives and drink a margarita. Elsie would serve them up and someone would get her head slapped over something stupid, probably Alma.

One day, I would be uprooted like a lonely tree in Louisiana to see Frankie again and we would dance and be free, eternally, like the Fourth of July.

Publications from Spinsters Ink

P.O. Box 242
Midway, Florida 32343
Phone: 800 301-6860
www.spinstersink.com

DISORDERLY ATTACHMENTS by Jennifer L. Jordan. 5th Kristin Ashe Mystery. Kris investigates whether a mansion someone wants to convert into condos is haunted. ISBN 1-883523-74-5 $14.95

VERA'S STILL POINT by Ruth Perkinson. Vera is reminded of exactly what it is that she has been missing in life.
ISBN 1-883523-73-7 $14.95

OUTRAGEOUS by Sheila Ortiz-Taylor. Arden Benbow, a motor-cycle riding, lesbian Latina poet from LA is hired to teach poetry in a small liberal arts college in northwest Florida.
ISBN 1-883523-72-9 $14.95

UNBREAKABLE by Blayne Cooper. The bonds of love and friend-ship can be as strong as steel. But are they unbreakable?
ISBN 1-883523-76-1 $14.95

ALL BETS OFF by Jaime Clevenger. Bette Lawrence is about to find out how hard life can be for someone of low society standing in the 1900s. ISBN 1-883523-71-0 $14.95

UNBEARABLE LOSSES by Jennifer L. Jordan. 4th in the Kristin Ashe Mystery series. Two elderly sisters have hired Kris to discover who is pilfering from their award-winning holiday display.
ISBN 1-883523-68-0 $14.95

FRENCH POSTCARDS by Jane Merchant. When Elinor moves to France with her husband and two children, she never expects that her life is about to be changed forever.

ISBN 1-883523-67-2 $14.95

EXISTING SOLUTIONS by Jennifer L. Jordan. 2nd book in the Kristin Ashe Mystery series. When Kris is hired to find an activist's biological father, things get complicated when she finds herself falling for her client. ISBN 1-883523-69-9 $14.95

A SAFE PLACE TO SLEEP by Jennifer L. Jordan. 1st in the Kristin Ashe Mystery series. Kris is approached by well known lesbian Destiny Greaves with an unusual request. One that will lead Kris to hunt for her own missing childhood pieces.

ISBN 1-883523-70-2 $14.95

THE SECRET KEEPING by Francine Saint Marie. The Secret Keeping is a high stakes, girl-gets-girl romance, where the moral of the story is that money can buy you love if it's invested wisely.

ISBN: 1-883523-77-X $14.95

WOMEN'S STUDIES by Julia Watts. With humor and heart, Women's Studies follows one school year in the lives of these three young women and shows that in college, one,s extracurricular activities are often much more educational that what goes on in the classroom. ISBN: 1-883523-75-3 $14.95

A POEM FOR WHAT'S HER NAME by Dani O'Connor. Professor Dani O'Connor had pretty much resigned herself to the fact that there was no such thing as a complete woman. Then out of nowhere, along comes a woman who blows Dani's theory right out of the water. ISBN: 1-883523-78-8 $14.95